(A twisted love story)

Revenge Mistaken

Jennifer Osuna Ausa

 FriesenPress

One Printers Way
Altona, MB R0G 0B0
Canada

www.friesenpress.com

ISBN
978-1-03-913855-1 (Hardcover)
978-1-03-913854-4 (Paperback)
978-1-03-913856-8 (eBook)

1. FICTION, ROMANCE

Distributed to the trade by The Ingram Book Company

13 JULY 2023

♡ REDOLFO

Enjoy Reading !!!

1

IT WAS THE FIRST DAY of autumn, though it wasn't proper sweater weather yet. Ivy Reynolds was overjoyed to feel the return of the crisp and cool days. It was a great time to sort through her wardrobe and get rid of her summer clothes along with items that she hadn't worn in too long. Soothing jazz music drifted from her speaker, warming her heart.

She found her scarves and felt delighted knowing that she could wear them again through fall until winter. She grinned when she saw the scarf that she knitted for Vins, her husband of five years.

Their bedroom smelled like a working bakeshop; they both love the scent of vanilla and cinnamon sugar. Ivy was so engrossed in her cleaning that she didn't realize until late that Vins had not come home for the weekend. He had told her that he was at a conference during the week but hadn't called to check in about staying late.

This is way out of character for Vins. It was the first time in five years that Ivy had felt deceived or betrayed. She couldn't pinpoint what had changed. She stopped cleaning and dialed Vins's mobile number. Her call went through his voicemail:

Vins here, please leave me a message and I will call you the moment I'm available.

"Hey hun, what's up? Please call me at home. I love you," Ivy said.

Then she hung up the phone. Emptiness enveloped her; she felt weak and fell onto a sofa inside her walk-in closet. Her heart was beating like

1

crazy. Ever since they got married, Ivy and Vins agreed that no matter how busy they were with their respective jobs, weekends were to be spent with each other. Her woman's intuition was on high alert, and she didn't like it. Because she was a strong-willed person, confident and full of self-esteem no matter what came her way, she stayed calm and focused. Not once did she allow her emotions to jump to conclusions without knowing the truth.

Waiting for Vins's explanation was the best thing to do. Her husband was a very punctual and honest person. No matter where he was in the world, he never failed to inform Ivy of his whereabouts. Even if he was rushing to a meeting from an airport in a foreign land, he would see to it that Ivy knew where he was. He was as reliable as clockwork.

Walking back and forth in their spacious living room in the autumn night, Ivy decided to stop worrying and keep herself busy. She went to the kitchen and prepared to cook their meal, hoping Vins would show up for dinner. Their kitchen was well-equipped, and they always kept their pantry full. Her only request when they started to build this house was a walk-in pantry. It was just like having a mini grocery store in her kitchen. Vins loved vegetables and seafood. After washing the broccoli, Ivy steamed it. She broiled salmon and cut lemon wedges. After cooking, she went to the washroom, filled the bathtub with hot water, and put her favorite essential oil in. She liked the mixture of lavender, orange, and bergamot scents. This mixture made her relaxed and at peace.

She went to the closet and got her favourite nightgown ready beside the tub. As she slipped into the bath, she reminisced about wonderful times she had spent with Vins. She could still feel the lingering touch of him. Her life was perfect with him, or so she thought.

The next day, Sunday, she woke up early hoping to see Vins beside her, but she was alone in their king size bed. She never imagined that this day would come, and she felt that her life was over. Terrified, she dialed Vins's number, but it went through to his voicemail again. She sighed and said, "Where is he this time?" After having her coffee, Ivy changed into her workout clothes, took her phone and house key, and went outside for her morning run. Ivy and Vins both loved to run, and this was the first time Ivy was running without her husband. While running, she saw Drew and Eve, another couple on their morning run. Eve was staring at her with a smirk on her face as if she knew something.

"Why are you running alone, where is Vins?" asked Eve. Ivy was startled, but remained composed and replied, "He's out of town this weekend, thank you for asking."

Drew and Eve said, "Oh" in unison. They wanted to chat further, but they decided to say goodbye, realizing that Ivy was not in her usual mood. Normally, she was cheerful and smiled a lot. But today she was aloof, her eyes weary.

The thought of being alone never crossed Ivy's mind because growing up she was surrounded with people who loved her dearly. Her parents were both retired and spending their time on their fifty-acre orchard in the valley. They often invited Ivy and Vins to visit but they always declined due to their hectic schedules. She had an older brother who doted on and protected her. Ethan lived overseas and was having the best time of his life; he was a professional car racer. Every time he traveled, he brought Ivy miniature cars and other car accessories as souvenirs. Because of that, Ivy started to love cars too. She was one of the best women car drivers in the city. Driving was like having her freedom in her hands.

One day, Vins told Ivy that he was planning to get a personal driver for her because he was not comfortable with her driving long distances. But Ivy instantly declined. Driving was therapeutic for her. Vins felt unappreciated and Ivy always had the last say. As a co-owner of Top Fashion Atelier, a fashion company that she and her best friends established after college, Ivy was always on the go. Her adventurous trips took up most of her time. Ivy had good eyes for the finest materials and products around the world. She even drove eight hours after a ten-hour flight just to experience silk harvesting. Seeing that moment made her heart skip a beat. It was like glancing at your high school crush at school after spring break. Ivy met her VIP client for the first time during that trip.

Suddenly, Ivy snapped back from her reverie. She stopped running and felt confused about why her husband was not home. She couldn't find anything wrong. In her mind, they were happy, secure, content, and always trusted each other. They knew everything about each other's lives, no secrets, no hidden agendas. But today was different. She headed home, took a shower, and had breakfast. She prepared herself to go to mass alone for the first time in five years. Inside the church, Ivy thought the priest's homily was directed to her. "You will never be alone, God is always with you," he said.

Ivy did not notice that tears were running down her cheeks and her hands were trembling nonstop. She clasped her hands together to lessen the shaking. When her soft sob was heard, people glanced in her direction and were curious. The lady beside her gave her a tissue. Ivy thanked her. After the mass, she stayed longer than usual in the pew. Ivy was sitting at an empty church; she could hear her own breathing and smell the scent of candles and flowers lingering around the church. This was her safe place. Her devotion was stronger than ever. But why did she feel abandoned with this strange feeling in her heart? Was she doubting God? She felt ashamed and looked at the crucifix in front of her. She asked the Lord to forgive her. Ivy wanted to clear her head of those thoughts and surrender all her emotions to God.

Time passed. The priest was on his way back inside the church to lock the door when he saw Ivy kneeling with her head bowed. He walked towards her to tell her that the church would be closed soon. But upon staring at her intently when she gazed at him, the priest saw her eyes without emotions, as if he could see through her soul. He stopped in his tracks and was about to leave to give her more time to contemplate when he heard her speaking.

"Father, I think God is punishing me?"

The priest was startled but decided to walk back towards her and sat behind her. He asked her, "Why did you say that?" He spoke in a calm tone and was feeling concern for the lady in front of him.

Ivy looked at the priest and just like the sacrament of confession, she told him about what's been happening over the past twenty-four hours. She even told him that it was the first time in five years that

4

her husband missed going to mass with her. Sunday church was a must for their family.

She was at loss, and she felt like their world had started to crumble. Then the priest asked her, "Do you trust the Lord?" Ivy wanted to say yes, but she couldn't say the word; her eyes just stared at the crucifix. She prayed to God to answer that question for her.

Ivy left the church with nowhere to go except home. But she did not want to go home. She still had no way to contact her husband. She missed the way he smelled.

2

A WEEK PASSED. IVY CALLED Samantha and Billy and asked them to meet her at the café where they used to hang out during their university days. Sam and Billy were her two best friends. They had been helping her to locate Vins over the past week. But to no avail.

Even Mama Belle, Vins's mom, was worried sick when she realized that Vins did not come home. She assured Ivy that when the right time came, her son would go back home. She knew her son was stubborn and had a mind of his own. But his love for Ivy was unconditional; it was like their hearts beat as one. He would never be unfair towards her.

Ivy's family had no idea about the incident. She wanted to shield them from pain, and she didn't want them to hate Vins.

When she reached the café, Billy walked towards her after she got out from her car. His emotions were like a roller coaster ride. Ivy had lost so much weight after just a week. Ivy hugged him; he kissed her forehead in return. They entered the café and found Sam sitting at their favorite spot.

"How I wish I could take away some of your burdens, babe," said Sam. She embraced Ivy. Naturally, Billy embraced the two special women in his life. He treated them as his siblings. They had grown up together and went to the same school until high school. At university,

Ivy and Sam took Design and Billy finished a degree in Computer Technology. They were together for every milestone.

Five years ago, it was the best time of their lives.

In January of that year, Sam got engaged to Robby Smithe. It was love at first sight. Robby was a hopeless romantic and wanted to seal the deal as soon as possible. After two months of dating, he proposed. Ivy and Billy were shocked but they saw that Sam was so happy, so they supported the marriage. Now Sam and Robby had a three-year-old daughter, Brianna.

June of that same year, Vins and Ivy had their church wedding. It was a small celebration with family and close friends. Vins planned the wedding to the tee. He told Ivy to choose her wedding gown and his tuxedo. Mama Belle was over the moon during her son's wedding. She couldn't stop crying thinking about her deceased husband. She knew that Vins would be a good husband and father because his dad was a wonderful person. It was different for Ivy's family; they had reservations about the wedding. They loved Vins the moment Ivy introduced him to them two years prior, but they felt there was something different about him that they couldn't pinpoint. Mommy Nas and Daddy Todd had been married for thirty-five years. They still behaved like teenagers; always bickering. But at the end of the day, they kissed and made up. They had no doubt that Ivy was crazy in love with Vins, so they kept quiet about how they felt about him.

August came, and Billy, Ivy, Sam, and Robby were doing their annual camping trip near the lake around the valley. Vins stayed home; he said he wasn't into camping. He and Ivy had only been married for two months and were still in their honeymoon stage, but still, he declined. Ivy was upset but she couldn't force Vins to join them. She gave him space and thought he would follow her to the cabin. But that did not happen.

They prepared their gear for fishing in the nearby lake, which was extremely popular for trout. Suddenly, Billy's ex-girlfriend Molly showed up at their rented cabin holding two children. Everyone was surprised and waited for Billy's reaction. Then Molly introduced their children to Billy while waiting near the front door. They were twins: Shelly and Lucas, age two. Billy was stunned to the point that he almost collapsed. Sam was quick to hold him and help him sit.

Ivy walked towards the door and extended her hand to hold Lucas's hand, inviting Molly and the children to come inside. Robby then picked Shelly up and placed her on the sofa. Even though it was still summer, the weather was cool and breezy. The camp site was secluded and near the water. Thinking the kids might be cold, Ivy prepared hot chocolate and gave it to them in the living room. Billy and Molly went outside and talked about their children.

Billy was so mad after Molly told him she intentionally kept him in the dark about his children's existence, and that she was leaving the kids in his care. She couldn't afford to support the children anymore and wouldn't take money from Billy. She had decided to live alone without her kids. Billy tried to calm down and solve the problem in a way that would be best for everyone. He had become a father instantly; he was delighted and terrified at the same time. No questions asked, just acceptance. No need for DNA testing; when he saw Shelly's face it was like looking in a mirror. As she got up to leave, Molly said, "May tenth, 2008: that's the day they were born." Then she left without even glancing at her kids.

Billy was at loss. How could he raise two toddlers on his own? He couldn't even look after himself. The moment Sam heard Molly's car leaving, she went outside to console Billy. As Billy wiped his tears, she patted his back affectionately as if to tell him that everything would be all right. They went inside; Robby gave Billy a brotherly hug. Robby loved everything about Sam. He knew the moment he and Sam got married that Billy and Ivy would be part of their lives. The three best friends were a pack. They couldn't break apart. After what felt like a century, Billy stepped forward and gave his twins a hug. "Shelly, Lucas, Daddy will always be here for you. I will never leave you and will always love you two." His best friends told the twins to call them Mom Ivy and Mama Sam. The twins smiled, still quiet, but they were not sad or feeling forsaken.

After spending another two days at the cabin, the friends decided to drive home.

When Ivy arrived home, she was happy to see Vins by the front door waiting for her.

"You are aware that we are still on our honeymoon, right? You should have stayed with me rather than spent it with your friends!" Vins confronted Ivy, he's mad, his brow furrowed.

"Hun, I asked you if you want to join us, but you declined, so I gave you space. We are doing this annual camping trip since way back when we were young, please don't be mad at me or at them." Ivy tried coaxing Vins, then held his hand and walked with him inside their home.

Ivy could feel he was so jealous of her friends; he knew they had both been a part of her life since childhood. Ivy never thought that he felt the need to compete for her attention. It never occurred to her that he's possessive. Her heart melted and she found it adorable.

"No more camping for you after this one if you want a successful marriage." Vins ordered Ivy while looking at her intensely. As for Vins, the moment he married Ivy, she belonged to him and only him, no matter what.

"If that will make you happy, I won't go with them again," Ivy replied while dragging herself to their bedroom and tried to avoid being confrontational.

3

IVY HEADED HOME AFTER SPENDING time with Sam and Billy. She was shocked when she saw the garage door was open and Vins was loading his truck with his personal stuff. Ivy immediately ran towards the garage, leaving her car door open and the engine still running. Vins was caught off-guard when he saw Ivy running towards his truck. He put down the boxes that he was holding and stood still, waiting for Ivy to stop.

"Hun, where have you been? How are you, have you eaten?" Ivy was overjoyed to finally see her husband and hugged his waist tightly. "You scared me. Please don't ever do that again," Ivy said, her heart exploding with love.

But to her surprise, Vins didn't move; he just stood there without even holding her. Reality struck; Ivy loosened her embrace and looked at Vins. She heard him speak.

"Let's get a divorce!"

It was not even a question; it was a direct instruction. Ivy panicked; her calm demeanor vanished. She almost shouted at Vins.

"Why are you divorcing me? I am your wife, for heaven's sake! We never quarrel, we never fight, we do not even get jealous. We have lived a happy married life for the past five years. What changed, Vins?"

She was panting as she said the last words; she couldn't take it anymore. She needed to hear his answer immediately.

As if he hadn't heard anything she said, Vins went to get Ivy's car and parked it in the garage, then closed the gate behind him. He had thought he would leave Ivy tonight, but seeing her like this, he couldn't do it. He felt a stab in his heart when he looked at his wife. She was desperate, but why? Vins thought that Ivy was a strong person; he had not seen this side of her when they were together.

Throughout their relationship, Vins had thought that Ivy never cared. She was not clingy the way he wanted her to be. When they started dating, he was drawn to her jolly and carefree personality. He loved everything about her then. He thought he would spent the rest of his life with her. But he had been wanting more without telling Ivy; she had no idea how he felt. He thought his actions would speak louder than words.

Ivy was unaware that she was walking towards the house without waiting for Vins. She went to the kitchen and got a bottled water. Her throat was dry from too much shouting. She never yelled or shouted and always spoke softly. She brought her water to the living room and sat on the sofa, her heart empty. Her self-esteem vanished as she thought about everything Vins had said.

Ivy had no idea how she slept that night. The next day she stayed in bed until dusk, thankful that it was Saturday. Vins stayed and slept in the guest room. He ordered lunch without even asking Ivy what she wanted. Their home phone rang; it was Mama Belle on the other line.

"Hello," Vins said. Mama Belle started crying when she heard her son's voice. She couldn't utter a word, she just listened.

Suddenly Vins said, "Mama, can you come over?" The moment he asked, Mama Belle hung up the phone, grabbed her car keys, and drove two hours to her son's house. Her son never sounded like this. It was almost night when Mama Belle arrived. She had a tough time driving because it was raining hard. Nervousness enveloped her mind; she focused on her driving and tried to stop thinking about her son.

Mama Belle felt relieved when she parked her car behind Vins's truck. He opened the front door when he saw his Mama get out of her car. Her coat was drenched; she had no umbrella in her car. She was wearing a pink sweater with a rainbow print under her brown coat.

She looked so young for her age. She had paired the sweater with slim brown pants and ankle boots. She brought an overnight bag because she was staying for the night and wanted to speak with the couple. She had always treated Ivy like her own child.

Vins gave his Mama a hug and escorted her inside. Ivy had no idea that Mama Belle was downstairs. She had been in bed all day. Her hair was uncombed, and her nightdress was a mess. She didn't have the willpower to leave the bed. The feeling of being unwanted and worthless consumed her. She had been full of confidence, but now her self-esteem was at its lowest. Every cell in her body was malfunctioning, and she couldn't think straight anymore. It was like her world was torn into pieces.

When Mama Belle went inside the house, her first instinct was to go to the kitchen. She cooked chicken soup with gnocchi and made toast. She looked at Vins as if to ask where Ivy was. Vins pointed his hand towards the ceiling.

Mama Belle decided to walk upstairs and knock-on Ivy's door. When she reached the second floor, she couldn't hear any movement in the bedroom. She didn't want to barge in and decided to wait for Ivy to come downstairs instead.

By that time, Ivy was taking a shower. Her tears were flowing, mixing with the water from the shower head. When she got out, she dried herself, put on warm clothes, and decided to go downstairs to finally talk to Vins about the divorce. Ivy did not want to harbor ill feeling towards her husband. For her, divorce was out of the question. She would fight to save their marriage no matter what. She strode downstairs, but when she heard Mama Belle's voice, Ivy started to sob.

When Mama Belle saw Ivy, she went to her, she hugged then consoled her. Ivy was sobbing uncontrollably, her eyes swollen. Vins told Mama Belle to let Ivy eat, since she had not eaten since breakfast. Mama Belle led Ivy to the dining table. Ivy was having a hard time swallowing, but she tried to get something down. She ate the soup and bread, then she pushed away the bowl in front of her and drank water.

Ivy and Vins stared at each other without blinking. Mama Belle saw the tension between them and about to leave to give them time to talk, but Ivy told her to stay. Her mother-in-law must know what was happening with their marriage and how Vins was treating Ivy.

"I never loved you from the start," Vins blurted out. Surprised, Mama Belle was the first to confront her son. "What are you saying? Everyone knows you love Ivy more than your life. You adore your wife!" Ivy held Mama Belle's hand.

Ivy was shocked with what Vins said that he never loved her from the start. That was the answer she's been waiting for. She couldn't forget about their first pregnancy, Vins deliberately sexually assaulted her when she was eight weeks pregnant, resulting to an early miscarriage; Ivy felt like she had been struck by lightning, it happened early on their marriage. During that time, Ivy was confused why Vins was so rough on her. He assaulted her because he didn't love her? Ivy asked herself in her mind over and over again. She had no idea back then, and now she had gotten her answer. From the start, she never reached his heart. Her hands were cold as ice due to shock. She wanted to throw up and her head hurt.

After that night, Ivy's life was never the same again. She cried her heart out, mourning the loss of the baby. She felt like she was losing her grip, Ivy thought that her husband loved her.

Ivy had always wanted to start a family with Vins, but he had never been into it. Ivy saw now that Vins had wanted out, even from the early days of their marriage. But even though he had caused her so much pain, Ivy wanted to stay. Was she selfish? She was afraid to be judged for getting a divorce and hoped her broken heart would eventually mend.

4

IT HAD BEEN A MONTH since Vins agreed to stay and work to save their marriage. He had felt so alone seeing Mama Belle console Ivy when he tried to leave. Mama Belle had left the next day, hoping that Vins and Ivy would mend their broken relationship. She knew that it was normal for couples to go through difficult phases.

Vins and Ivy slept in the same room but never had an intimate moment. Ivy realized that they had not touched each other since her second miscarriage. That was a year ago.

Had they fallen out of love because they were both so busy and focused on their careers? Ivy recalled that when they started dating, they were physically in sync. They were compatible, and their intimacy was intense. The bedroom was the only place where they became one. Just by looking at each other they knew what was to come. Ivy loved Vins so much that she agreed to do everything for him. She realized that sex was the only thing she and Vins loved doing together. That was it.

Still, she knew that her love for Vins would last for a lifetime. After all, she had given something up just to make Vins happy: her friendship with Sam and Billy.

Vins had only joined Ivy once on her adventures: a trip to Thailand. He said he wanted to see the elephants.

Elephants? He cared more about elephants than about spending time with Ivy. After that trip, he did all his international travel by himself, as part of his trading business. They had also gone to Italy once to visit Mama Belle's family in Naples. *Those were our best travel memories,* Ivy thought. Since then, they had never bothered each other about their business or their travels. They never talked about the future, never discussed having children.

The month Vins was home after asking for divorce, Ivy wanted to seek marriage counselling, but Vins declined. He had already decided that the moment Ivy realized that their differences were irreconcilable, he would leave. He never tried to save the marriage. He felt suffocated, confused. Every time he was with Ivy, he felt disgusted and annoyed, and wanted to be far away from her.

The week that he disappeared, Vins had visited the Lakehouse that he bought through his realtors, Drew and Eve. He bought the house last spring, and it should have been his fifth wedding anniversary gift to Ivy.

He hadn't planned to leave that day; he thought he was just taking a day trip to the house to see if it was move-in ready. His plan has been to surprise his wife with her dream home. But then something snapped in his mind. He drove to the village, bought food, clothes, and other necessities. He felt alive and excited. He wanted to call Ivy but stopped himself.

The first night away from his wife was hard for him. In his mind, this was not what he wanted. But his heart was telling him otherwise. He got a voicemail from Ivy the following day and decided not to call her back. He wanted to explore this new life. It was fun cooking breakfast just for himself. Nobody bothered him. He felt he had gotten his freedom back. This was the life he wanted, away from the city, exploring the small town near Ivy's dream home. But he didn't want Ivy here. Puzzled about his feelings toward his wife, Vins shook his head, trying to clear his mind. He couldn't imagine Ivy in this house.

Vins was lost; he couldn't explain his emotions. Was he meant to live with Ivy? Or was he better off alone? After a week of soul searching, Vins decided he would go back to Ivy and ask her for divorce. Plain and simple.

His life without his wife was what he wanted, and it would be the best thing he could do for himself. He knew that his wife was a strong woman, and she would understand his decision because she loved him so much. Her priority was always his happiness. So, he thought.

When he reached the city and was about to enter their front gate, Vins parked his car and stared at their house. He felt at loss; from the moment he asked Ivy for her hand in marriage, this was the house that he wanted them to live in. Vins looked for an answer from within himself, but he couldn't find anything wrong. He just wanted to get out of this prison-like home.

His time spent with Ivy was always happy. They never fought or got mad at each other. Whenever Vins was irritable, Ivy always understood where he was coming from. She gave him space to let out his anger then calmly explained her point of view. They never raised their voices; they gave each other time to express their feelings. That was one of the best characteristics of their marriage.

5

IVY KNEW THAT SHE HAD to do what was best for herself. She wanted to be in control of her life again. Healing was still far away, but she could work to rebuild her self-esteem and self-confidence.

She thought about a dream she'd had a year ago. In her dream, she was holding her baby girl; the baby looks like Vins. Ivy's heart was overflowing with emotions, and she could smell the scent of baby powder. Was this for real? When she woke up, she felt pain in her pelvis and discomfort in her belly. She was fourteen weeks pregnant, her second pregnancy.

The moment she had found out that she was having a baby, she felt alive and full of energy. When she told Vins about her pregnancy, he was ecstatic and hugged her tightly. But after that, he refused to make any plans or talk about the pregnancy at all.

The morning when she awoke from her dream she's in pain, she got up and about to stand, but her legs felt wobbly. She fell on the floor; she was so scared. Her head was spinning, her body was in so much pain, everything was fading. While holding her belly, she saw fresh blood in her nightdress. Panicked, she screamed for help, thinking Vins was home. But nobody answered her call. She dialed his cell, but it was turned off. She was home alone. She was afraid that she might lose her baby again. Ivy decided to call Billy. She was worried that he might not answer; she hadn't seen Billy in four years, since their last camping trip with Samantha. Although Sam and Billy were the two most important people in her life, she had decided to stop seeing them to make Vins happy.

Vins had asked her to choose between him and her two best friends the moment she stepped inside their home after their camping trip. She was stunned by his abrupt order. She stared at him; his face was red, and his eyes were full of hatred. Ivy was so tired, so she just said, "Okay." She soon realized that she had made a terrible mistake, but it was too late.

Still, Ivy felt that she had no choice; she gathered her strength and dialed Billy's mobile number. He answered after one ring.

"Hello?"

"I'm sorry Billy, but can you come over now? I think I'm losing my baby again, please hurry," Ivy told him.

Billy was in shock; he couldn't explain his emotions. All he could say was, "Alright." Then he put his twins in the car and drove to Ivy's house as fast as he could.

Before getting into the car, Billy had called 911 and instructed them to send an ambulance to Ivy's address. He told the dispatcher about the call he got from his best friend. He couldn't explain the severity of Ivy's condition because he had no idea that she was pregnant. When he arrived at Ivy's door, Billy could hear sirens close by. Ivy called to him the moment she heard the front door open.

"I am upstairs in our bedroom," Ivy yelled.

Billy ran towards Ivy's master bedroom, instructing the twins to wait for the paramedics and police.

He saw Ivy sitting down near the bed holding her belly, looking pale and helpless. She was crying nonstop. He could see blood on her clothes. She tried her best to smile for Billy; she felt relieved that he was here. He held her hands and kissed her forehead.

"Please wait a little longer, the paramedics are just around the corner now!" Billy told Ivy. "Mom Ivy is upstairs, when you reach the second floor please turn right and walk straight, you will see her bedroom," Lucas told the paramedics when they arrived.

The paramedics gave Ivy first aid, instructing Billy to prepare her things; they were going to transport her to the nearest hospital. Billy followed their instructions and grabbed whatever he thought Ivy might need. He called Samantha and told her that he would drop off his twins with her before going to the hospital to be with Ivy.

When they arrived at Sam's house, she was ready to go with Billy and asked Robby to look after the three kids on their behalf. As Billy drove towards the hospital, he explained to Sam what had happened to Ivy. Then he instructed Sam to call Vins. Sam dialed Vins's mobile number, but his phone was turned off. She called Ivy's parents and informed them of Ivy's whereabouts. Then she called Mama Belle.

Upon reaching the hospital, Billy and Sam proceeded to the front desk and inquired about Ivy Reynolds. The receptionist checked her computer and found that Ivy was still in the emergency room. Billy and Sam went to the ER and sat in the waiting area. After an hour, the ER doctor came out and called for Ivy Reynolds's family. "Here, we're Ms. Reynolds family!" Billy said.

The ER doctor told them that Ivy and the baby were safe but need to stay in the hospital to be monitored. Knowing that Ivy and her child were well, Sam and Billy were relieved. When the doctor left, they hugged each other. Before Ivy was wheeled into a regular room, Mama Belle arrived. She drove as fast as she could after she got a call from Sam. The moment Sam, Billy, and Mama Belle entered Ivy's room, Mama Belle arranged the things that Billy had brought and checked if Ivy needed something, offering to drive to Ivy's home or just buy whatever she needed.

When Ivy was transferred in the private room and she saw her mother-in-law and her best friends, she started crying. Ivy was afraid to face them because she had almost lost her baby. She was in too much pain thinking about it. Sam held her left hand and Billy held her right hand. Mama Belle felt guilty that her son was not here; he was unaware of what had happened to his wife. She was so embarrassed to look at her daughter-in-law.

Ivy reached out to Mama Belle. She could see from Mama Belle's eyes that she felt sorry for Ivy. But it was not her fault if her son was not there. Mama Belle cried the moment she held Ivy's hand. She couldn't control her emotions and she gave Ivy a hug. She wished that her daughter-in-law had never experienced this pain.

Billy and Sam left the moment Ivy was settled and sleeping. They told Mama Belle that they would be back tomorrow. Both were heartbroken to see Ivy's condition.

The next day, Vins was still nowhere in sight. Mama Belle decided to call his assistant, Jessie. "Hi Jessie, this is Vins's mother, do you have any idea where my son is? Please tell him to call me as soon as possible." Then she thanked Jessie and hung up.

Jessie walked towards Vins's office. He had been staying there for the past two nights, and he was enraged. When Jessie knocked on the door, Vins yelled at her to go away. Scared of her boss, she did not open the door; she told Vins in a loud voice that his mom had called, and he needed to call her back as soon as possible. Vins was puzzled about why his mother called him. He waited until he had calmed down a bit more and dialed her number.

"Hi, Mama!" Vins said when his mom answered his call on the first ring. The moment Mama Belle heard Vins's voice, she yelled at him and asked him why he had turned off his cell phone. She had been calling him since yesterday. Vins was stunned and speechless because Mama Belle never raised her voice, even when she was mad at him. This was a first.

Mama Belle was also surprised with her outburst and tried to compose herself. When she was in control of her emotions, she told Vins what had happened to Ivy. Vins felt furious all over again. He blamed Ivy for what was happening to them. He was angry because for the past two days, his wine bottle production had been halted due to mechanical problems. He had stayed at the plant office to look after the damages and supervise his staff while they repaired the machine. They needed to deliver five thousand wine bottles in two weeks' time. He didn't want to delay this order from one of his best clients. Vins wondered why every time Ivy was pregnant something bad happened to his business.

During their first pregnancy, he had lost the biggest order in his career. That time, the client told him that they cancelled their purchase order because they found a supplier with a lower price. The client paid him for the breach of contract. Vins was so furious that he almost broke his office window. He went ballistic. When he got home that night, he walked straight to the master bedroom. He saw Ivy sitting at her study table. He grabbed her, threw her on the bed, and tried to undress her aggressively.

"Please do not do this to me, it is unsafe for the baby, I feel sick, and I am nauseous," Ivy pleaded. But Vins wanted to take revenge on her. He felt that Ivy and the baby had brought him bad luck. He succeeded in being intimate with Ivy.

After, Ivy cried nonstop; she felt violated and abused. She couldn't explain why Vins had done it. Ivy didn't tell anyone about what happened; she couldn't hate Vins. Maybe he was in trouble or something. Vins was not remorseful; instead, he felt that he had achieved his purpose. He even left the house after that and went for a drink at his favorite bar.

On her second night in the hospital, Ivy asked the nurse to give her a bath. She felt sticky and unclean. Her body was recovering, and a good bath would make a big difference.

Her obstetrician visited her that morning and checked her chart then told her the bleeding was controlled and the fetus was safe. When the nurse walked in, she helped Ivy to the bathroom. Ivy was glad that after two days she could finally take a bath. The nurse washed Ivy's hair then let Ivy wash her own body. After, Ivy tried her best to put on her clothes. As the nurse walked her back to her bed, she felt a stabbing pain in her abdomen.

Mama Belle screamed when she saw blood on the floor, flowing from between Ivy's legs. The nurse helped Ivy into her bed then pushed the emergency button to call for assistance. The vaginal bleeding was getting heavier, and Ivy's temperature was rising. When the obstetrician walked in, she instructed her staff to bring Ivy to the delivery room. Her diagnosis was critical. Earlier her check-up was good; what had happened?

A dilation and curettage (D&C) procedure was done at once; the doctor couldn't control the heavy vaginal bleeding. Mama Belle was the one who gave the authorization to proceed with the D&C. They couldn't save the baby. Ivy was white as a sheet after the procedure.

When Ivy woke up in the recovery room, she found out that she had lost the baby. If hearing a scream could kill, all the people inside the room would be dead. The doctor gave her something to calm her nerves.

6

IT WAS ON IVY'S THIRD day in the hospital that Vins finally showed up. Billy couldn't control his emotions and punched Vins in the face. He was furious with Vins for causing Ivy so much pain. The atmosphere in the room was intense, and Vins could only blame himself. Billy, Sam, and Mama Belle felt that Vins had intentionally neglected Ivy during this crisis. Sam intervened; she pulled Billy far away from Vins and whispered, "It's not worth it."

Mama Belle slapped Vins in the face. She couldn't control herself and continued to hit him hard all over his body. Vins didn't flinch. He ignored the pain, gazing at Ivy. For a second, he felt sorry for her. After a while, though, he became angry once again. He didn't show it on his face, but deep inside, he was mad as hell. He blamed Ivy for her misfortune because she didn't take care of her body and their baby. That was what she got for always being on the go, and for being too self-centered. He couldn't explain why he hated her so much.

Ivy stared at Vins, feeling bad for him. She couldn't blame Billy and Mama Belle for hitting him. She wanted to curse him, but her heart said otherwise. Her love for Vins was strong and she couldn't afford to lose him. She reached out to Vins; she wanted him to console her during this darkest hour. But he did not move. He gazed sharply at Ivy, but she ignored it.

"I lost the baby again. I'm so sorry, hun!"

23

When Sam, Billy, and Mama Belle heard her, they looked at each other in disbelief. They left the room to give Ivy and Vins some privacy. Billy held Mama Belle's hands and apologized for hitting Vins. He had never doubted Vins's affection for Ivy. That's why he had agreed to not see Ivy anymore when she told him about Vins's jealousy.

She had begged Billy to give Vins time to accept their relationship. So, they decided to stop seeing each other in the meantime, though they continued communicating by phone or video chatting when Vins was not around. In Billy's opinion, she earned some small form of communication for being so loyal to Vins. Imagine, four years of not seeing Ivy. Before her marriage, they were together almost every day.

Billy had never heard Ivy complain about her relationship with her husband. He thought they were stronger than ever. Every time they spoke on the phone, Ivy was still the same bubbly and cheerful person she had always been, giggling most of the time. Her weekly video calls with the twins were her happiest moments. She showered them with gifts.

As for Sam, she and Ivy had never stopped seeing each other. The only difference in their relationship was that they spent less time chatting over coffee after work. During Sam's maternity leave, Ivy had kept herself busy with the help of Hannah, her assistant of the past three years. Her usual monthly adventure trips decreased to quarterly travel. Ivy became hands-on with her business dealings. She could easily navigate her transactions with suppliers around the world via email and video calls.

When it came time for Brianna's baptism, Ivy and Vins attended the church ceremony. Ivy served as Brianna's godmother. After church, they did not join in the reception. Ivy saw a glimpse of Billy in the church but didn't get a chance to talk to him because Vins was in a hurry dragging Ivy out by her wrist. Vins always said that Ivy and Billy would never be together again.

Mama Belle accepted Billy's apology and she told him that she was also sorry for her son's behaviour. She couldn't think of a reason for Vins to abandon Ivy during this crucial time of their lives. She was longing to have grandchildren, imagining what the kids would look like. She was looking forward to hearing them call her "grandmama."

Sam and Vins's relationship was like oil and water; Ivy could never leave them in a room together. Sam hated Vins to the core, especially when Ivy told her that Vins was forcing Ivy to end her friendship with Billy and limit her friendship with Sam. Sam loved Ivy so much that she agreed to go along with Vins's wishes.

She told Robby about Vins's demands happened when he picked her up from work that day. His response was eye-opening.

"Some people are possessive and declare ownership of their partner. Even if it's one-sided, I can see that Vins loves Ivy unconditionally. Remember how I cried during their wedding? I saw in Vins's eyes that he adores Ivy so much, and I think Ivy reciprocates his love for her. When two people acknowledge and accepted each other, they tend to bind together. They allow their partner to be a part of their lives no matter what. I can't judge their lives, but I can't deny the fact that Vins neglected Ivy this time. If I was in his shoes, the moment I learned about your pregnancy I would give my full attention to you to avoid a miscarriage. But I am not Vins. As for you, my wife, please give him the benefit of the doubt. Even if you love Ivy, you can't side with her. Let them solve their own problems and control your emotions. We can watch them from afar, listen if they want to unload their thoughts, but we should never give unsolicited advice. We have our own problems to deal with." Sam didn't say anything but took her husband's words to heart.

On her sixth day in the hospital, Ivy's doctor gave her a discharge slip and told her she was ready to go home. Her husband went to the cashier counter and paid her hospital bill. Mama Belle packed Ivy's bags and put the flowers her friends had sent in the back of the car.

A nurse wheeled Ivy out of the hospital in a wheelchair. Mama Belle walked behind them. Vins went ahead to get his car and parked it near the hospital entrance. He helped Ivy out of the wheelchair and into the car. On the way home, he drove a little slower than usual so that Ivy wouldn't be uncomfortable.

He carried Ivy into the house princess-style. She felt loved and appreciated in that moment. She leaned her head on Vins's chest and his warm body gave her goosebumps. His signature scent made her feel safe and secure. Even Vins felt different; he loved Ivy just like before. When Mama Belle saw the loving couple, she hoped and prayed that they would start a new life after the tragic incident. She wished that they would be together forever. Vins put his wife into the recliner in the living room.

Vins went out to help Mama Belle bring Ivy's stuff inside. Ivy's phone rang; it was Billy, asking her if she was home yet. After hanging up, Ivy told Mama Belle and Vins not to prepare lunch because Billy, the twins, and Sam's family were coming over, and they were bringing food. Ivy was standing firm in her decision. She would continue her friendship with Billy and Sam no matter what. Alarmed, Mama Belle immediately looked at Vins and watched for his reaction; he only nodded. Then he asked his wife if she wanted to go upstairs to change. She said yes, and Vins carried her to the bedroom. Vins was being so attentive to all of Ivy's needs. Even if he wasn't saying much, his actions spoke louder than his words. Ivy was loving the change in Vins, and she couldn't hide her smile.

Vins went downstairs after he had settled his wife. He told Mama Belle that he would set up the folding chairs and table on the terrace. Mama Belle helped him move the chairs and asked Ivy what colour she preferred for the tablecloth. Ivy told her what she wanted, and Mama Belle prepared the table; it was so beautiful under the canopy. The weather outside was warm but breezy. The table centrepiece was the flowers from the hospital.

Mama Belle put the bouquet in a crystal vase and re-arranged it to give a new look. Ivy chose the yellow tablecloth and asked Mama Belle to use the handmade plates that she and Vins had bought in Naples the last time they visited the city. The print was a mixture of blue, green, and yellow flowers. Vins even chilled his favorite wine, but this time Ivy was not allowed to drink. He smiled when he recalled times when Ivy had gotten drunk.

They had shared so many happy memories, and Vins tried to remember the good times, though he felt pain in his heart.

When Billy and Sam's families arrived, they were told they would be dining on the terrace outside the couple's bedroom to avoid Ivy straining her body by using the stairs. Billy and Robby transferred the food into a nice serving platter that Mama Belle had prepared earlier. They both held a tray in their hands as they made their way out to the terrace from the master bedroom.

When Vins saw the men, he grabbed the tray from Robby's hands and put it on the table, then he told Billy to put the other tray down, too. Both men hugged Vins once their hands were free. Ivy and Mama Belle were both teary-eyed when they saw the men hugging. Only Sam found it annoying. But she was hoping that one day, Vins would accept them as part of his family.

Their lunch went smoothly. Even Vins laughed as the three friends reminisced about their childhood mishaps and adventures. Even the kids found it hilarious; they couldn't imagine that their parents had been so crazy when they were young. Ivy held Vins's hand when he couldn't control his laughter. She found it amusing and homey at the same time.

Their home was never this loud and busy, but she was loving every second of it. This was the moment she had been waiting for: to see her husband finally open their home to her best friends. Never in her wildest dreams could she have imagined that everything Vins was doing was just for a show. After lunch, they played cards; Billy and Ivy were both hustlers when it came to playing poker. But who would have thought that a quiet and reserved person like Robby would be a such a sly player? Even Sam had no idea that her husband would win all the sets played. Vins sat beside Ivy, watching as his wife lost each game. He felt sorry for her. He kept touching her shoulder, sometimes massaging it. Ivy asked Vins to hold her cards; she wanted to go to the washroom. But she never expected that when she stood up, she would feel dizzy and almost faint. Vins hold her and helped her to the washroom. He told her to stop playing cards and helped her to lie down in bed.

"We should leave and let Ivy rest," Sam said. Mama Belle sent everyone to the door and thanked them for the wonderful lunch. After putting Ivy to bed, Vins helped his mama to clean up the table and put the leftover food into a container.

Before going downstairs, he walked toward the bed and checked on Ivy, who by now was sleeping peacefully on her side, hugging a long pillow that she had purchased recently. She looked pale but her beauty was still apparent. Vins wanted to caress her face, but he was scared to wake her up.

He left the room, leaving the door open a crack so that he could hear her if she needed anything. Vins needed to have a heart-to-heart talk with his mom about his decision regarding his marriage with Ivy.

7

IVY COULDN'T LIVE IN A house that never become a home. She couldn't love a person who had never loved her back. She couldn't change her life for someone who had never valued her worth. This was how Ivy felt when Vins left their home. She thought about cutting her wrists, but she never had the courage to do it. Her home became her sanctuary. She didn't open the door or answer the phone for a week, and she made sure that the door was double-locked so that nobody could come inside.

It was only when her parents and her brother paid her a visit that Ivy decided to open her door for them. Ivy lost her footing when she saw her family in her home. Ethan grabbed her before she fell to the ground. The family helped her to sit on the sofa. They gave their full attention to Ivy, who by that time was sobbing uncontrollably.

Mommy Nas never showed her how she was feeling and was always in control of her emotions. Daddy Todd was more emotional than his wife. His eyes were red, though he wasn't crying. His hands were shaking when he held Ivy by her shoulder. It was more difficult for Ethan; he felt rage and anger that wanted to escape from his body. He wanted to hit something or someone. Being an athlete, he was always in control of his action and emotions, but it was different today. His baby sister was his life, and she was in so much pain. His heart was crushed. "Do you want to stay with us in the valley for a while?"

Mommy Nas asked her daughter. Ivy declined and said that she would stay in her house and face her problem head on. She wanted to shield her family from this chaotic episode of her life.

During her two miscarriages, she had asked her family not to visit, because she couldn't bear for them to see her in such a difficult emotional state. She didn't want them to feel her pain. Her family always granted her wishes, so they never consoled her in person. But their hearts shattered into pieces when they learned she had lost her baby twice. They stayed with Ivy for three days, until she showed them that she was starting to feel normal again. During their last family dinner before they left for the valley, Daddy Todd asked Ivy what her plan now that Vins had left. Her parents offered to pay the mortgage in full as their birthday gift to her. That way she would have her own place. They would buy Vins out. Ivy was so grateful for her parents, and she accepted their offer because she wanted to keep the house, even if there were many sad memories that came with it.

As for Ethan, he invited his sister to join him at his next international competition in Singapore at the end of this summer. "It will be all expenses paid and will fly first class." Ethan said with a wink. Ivy punched her brother's arm while smiling and asked him if he was serious. She accepted his offer in a flash.

They continued chatting until midnight. Ivy coaxed Ethan into including their parents for the Singapore trip, and he agreed. The family of four would have something to look forward to this summer.

The next morning, Mommy Nas was making breakfast when she heard the front door open. It was Billy and the twins; she waved her hands and told them to come in.

Billy was embarrassed to find Ivy's family at her home. He hadn't told her he and the twins were coming over; he had wanted to surprise her. Mommy Nas thought Billy looked troubled, but she brushed it off and ignored the look.

She placed eggs, bacon, bagels, and cereal on the table and told the twins to eat. Billy grabbed milk from the fridge and served it warm for the twins. Daddy Todd and Ethan joined them, they were happy to see Billy and the twins. They were glad that Ivy would have someone by her side when they left. The men chatted while they waited for Ivy to come down. Billy was always a fan of Ethan; he was engrossed as he listened to stories about Ethan's racing experiences. Moments later, Ivy was running downstairs with her hair still wet from the shower. She was surprised to see that they had company for breakfast that morning. Billy stood up and waited for Ivy to sit in the chair beside him then gave her a kiss on the cheek. Ivy just stared at him; she thought his face looked gloomy. After everyone had sat down to eat their breakfast, Billy spoke.

"I have a huge favor to ask, Ivy. It's about the twins." Everyone were all ears. He continued. "I got this job offer from the east coast office for my dream job. I want to check out the area before I make any decisions to see if the neighbourhood is accessible to elementary schools and is suitable for raising the twins. Can I leave them here with you for a week or two while I'm there? Please?"

Billy held Ivy's hands, coaxing her to say yes. Mommy Nas was all smiles and excitedly told Ivy that it would be a good idea to help Billy and to have company at home. Daddy Todd and Ethan nodded in unison. Ivy then asked the twins if they wanted to stay with her while their Daddy checked out his new job. The twins agreed immediately and told their father that they would be respectful to Mom Ivy. The twins loved their Mom Ivy so much and always had a great time with her.

After breakfast, Ivy's family left for the valley. Ethan would be staying with his parents for the winter. He would be doing some winter driving in preparation for his competition in Singapore. Billy and the twins decided to go back home after they got Ivy's approval for the twins' upcoming visit. Billy was scheduled to leave for the east coast the following week. He would drop off the twins with Ivy the day before his flight.

8

TWO WEEKS PASSED. IVY HAD the best time of her life taking care of Shelly and Lucas. They enjoyed eating out, visiting the park, and shopping. Ivy worked from home when the twins were with her. She spent quality time with them while she worked to heal her body and mind in the wake of her separation from Vins. She let her assistant, Hannah, monitor the company's projects and deliveries. Ivy was so thankful for her assistant's dedication and passion for her job.

Ivy and the twins were about to go outside for a walk in the park when Hannah called her for an emergency meeting with their VIP client from the north coast. Mr. Thomas Roye was in town and wanted to check on the prototype fabrics for his next bulk orders. Ivy couldn't afford not to meet up with him, so she called Hannah and asked her to prepare the office and keep Mr. Roye entertained until she arrived.

Hannah knew that the twins would be coming so she set up an extra table and chairs near her work station for the kids to hang out until after the meeting. Samantha was also coming to the meeting, and she brought Brianna to play with the twins. Mr. Roye arrived at the Top Fashion Atelier office ahead of Ivy and Samantha. Hannah ushered him into Ivy's office and offered him a drink while he waited for Ivy and Sam. The office has a huge mahogany table that Ivy used as her desk. Behind the desk, there was a console table with framed pictures and some awards that Ivy had received. Her swivel chair was purple; the room was full of small pops of colour.

Tom looked at the pictures on the desk; Ivy at the silk harvest; Ethan at one of his races; Ivy at college with Billy and Sam; Mommy Nas and Daddy Todd; Ivy with a baby during christening; Ivy with a twin. When Ivy and the twins arrived, he heard the little girl called Ivy "Mom Ivy."

Ivy hurriedly entered her office and saw her guest's annoyed look. She was stunned to see Mr. Roye adjusting his tie as if to allow himself to breathe properly.

"You're one fine designer, Ms. Reynolds. I like your purple swivel chair, and the pops of colours in your office. By the way your photos gave me a glimpse of your life," said Tom while he extends his hand to Ivy. He's so excited to hold Ivy's hand even for a brief seconds.

"Thank you, Mr. Roye for the compliment," Ivy replied with a smile on her face and shook Tom's hand.

She called Hannah to inform Samantha that they will proceed with the meeting. The twins and Brianna stayed in Samantha's office after the meeting started.

Ivy showed Mr. Roye the prototype fabrics that she and her supplier from Turkey had created. Ivy felt satisfied that Mr. Roye had a smile on his face. Sam and Ivy were hoping that this was a done deal and that they could sign a contract. They invited Mr. Roye for lunch, and he agreed. The kids stayed with Hannah.

While they were eating and discussing their business deal, Ivy realized that Mr. Roye was staring at her. Even Samantha seemed to have noticed; she tried to interrupt Mr. Roye's gaze by asking if he wanted to order more. Ivy knew her best friend was always on guard and this guy would be in trouble if he made any inappropriate moves. Ivy couldn't hide her smirk when Sam pretended to choke on her food. That was the only time that Mr. Roye looked away from Ivy for the duration of the meal.

Billy arrived home the next day. They sat in Ivy's living room, and he told her that although he had been on cloud nine when he was offered the job, he was disappointed with what he saw when he got there, and he couldn't see himself living on the east coast; it was uninspiring and meaningless.

However, he had already contacted his realtor and put his town-house up for sale. He had decided that the job offer was his dream job and that he would accept it no matter what. After a week, the realtor had received an offer way over the asking price, and Billy had accepted. But now he was facing a dilemma; the job was not what he wanted. He and the twins needed a place to stay, because in a month's time, the new owner would take possession of the house.

Ivy laughed out loud at the thought of Billy and the twins being homeless. She offered to let her best friend rent her in-law suite while he looked for their new home. The in-law suite in the basement had its own full kitchen, a small dining-living area, two bedrooms, and one full bath. It also had its own private entrance and laundry. It was supposed to be Mama Belle's space if she decided to sell her old house. Vins had wanted his mama to live with them when the time came.

Billy was overjoyed and told Ivy to charge him a fair rent because she was a good landlady. Then they both laughed and called the twins to join them.

Ivy welcomed Billy and his twins when they moved in with her. During that period, Ivy started to heal herself and bonded well with her new housemates. Billy was indeed her best friend. They shared dinner once in a while and did some shopping together. When Ivy found out that Billy had found a new house, she asked if they still wanted to stay with her during the Christmas season. She wanted them to spend more time with her.

Billy bought a single detached home forty minutes away from Ivy's house. The house had three bedrooms plus a den and a huge back-yard. He spent all the money he got from the sale of his townhome to buy his new property.

On Christmas day, Sam's family joined Ivy, Billy, and the twins for lunch. The kids got their Christmas presents from Santa Claus, and they were so happy to receive so many gifts. Ivy's parents video called them, and they enjoyed watching the kids rummaging through their presents. Mama Belle also gave Ivy a call and asked Ivy to join her for New Year's Eve. Ivy declined; she already had plans to visit her family in the valley.

Ivy decided to stay away from Vins's family for the time being. She was longing for a pain-free holiday. In order to fully accept her fate, she had to heal herself. She was yearning to call Vins to wish him a Merry Christmas, but she suppressed her desire to talk to him. In her heart, Vins would forever be her husband. She still held out hope that Vins would realize he had made a mistake and come home.

Six months had passed since their separation and Vins had never called her. Ivy's heart ached, so she decided to visit him at his office. She thought that a surprise visit would be a good idea. She really missed him so much.

Her decision had been impulsive; she drove faster than usual because she wanted to see him right away. When she reached his office she could see the office door was ajar; she walked quickly in her excitement. When she got to the door she could hear Vins telling Jessie that he missed his family.

"Why not call your mom if you miss her?" asked Jessie.

"I miss my wife," Vins replied, sighing.

"I thought you missed your family. How can you say you miss Ivy? You don't even have a kid so you're not really family," Jessie said, laughing.

Ivy could feel Vin's love; her husband missed her too. But when she heard what Jessie said she felt as if her heart was being squeezed and she couldn't breathe properly. She knew that Vins was saying something, but her mind shut off and she couldn't make out the words. She started to step away from the door.

Her whole being was broken into pieces. Somehow, she made it home from Vin's office and threw herself onto the couch. The feeling of loneliness enveloped her as she hugged her knees to her chest.

9

AFTER THAT INCIDENT, IVY THREW herself into her work. She decided to grow their business and expanded her role to include purchasing as well as product development. She contacted her suppliers in Turkey and requested an update on the product that she had been developing over the past year, a sweater that used wool as soft as cashmere.

The moment the fabric was ready to be launched, she contacted her VIP Client Mr. Roye from the North coast and showed him the finished product via video call.

"The colors of the fabrics are amazing, and I love to feel how soft it would be. My hands are full at the moment and couldn't fly to your office" Mr. Roye said and added

"Could you bring the swatches to me, I would love to see it in person, my secretary will arrange your trip, Ms. Reynolds?" Tom was excited while asking Ivy but at the same time, he's not expecting a positive response from his supplier.

Ivy declined then said, "You don't have to do that Mr. Roye, I will arrange for my own trip and would love to show you our swatches together with a prototype. Hannah, my assistant will inform you about our itinerary the moment we booked our flights. I will bring her too during this trip." A travel to the North coast will be a breather Ivy thought. After they hung up the phone, Ivy instructed Hannah to arrange their flights, hotel, and car rental. They would fly to the north coast that Friday. She discussed her trip with Sam and told her to monitor the production in Turkey.

After landing up north, Ivy and Hannah drove to the hotel where they would share a suite. There were lots of fishing boats in the marinas and tourists were roaming around the city. Ivy and Hannah were excited to stay awake and explore after their meeting with Mr. Roye early the following morning.

When she woke up, Ivy was feeling proud of herself and the sweater prototypes that she would be presenting to her VIP client at nine a.m. Neither Ivy nor Hannah had slept well; good thing the hotel room had a coffee machine. Ivy chose a dark roast and added hazelnut creamer. Satisfied with her coffee, she placed the documents and fabric swatches into her briefcase.

Ivy took a shower and put on a crisp, white top paired with dark brown plaid pants and brown stilettos. She was still wearing her engagement and wedding rings on her left hand; she was a married woman until the divorce papers were signed. While looking in the mirror, she tried to steady her thoughts and brush off negative energy. She put on a little makeup and some nude lipstick. She wore the Omega watch that she had gotten from her parents after her university graduation.

Ivy felt a little nervous because this was the first time that she would be presenting her new fabric and prototype to her VIP client. She was praying that the meeting with Mr. Roye would be a success.

Mr. Roye's office was a twenty-minute drive outside the city center. The scenery along the highway was breathtaking. The snow-caps on the mountains were still visible even during summertime. Hannah was driving with a smile on her face and enjoying the fresh air, while Ivy was checking her emails on her tablet.

As they pulled into Mr. Roye's driveway they passed a huge farm-house-style home with a front porch that could fit twenty lounge chairs, surrounded by a well-maintained lawn. This was Mr. Roye's estate. Hannah followed the sign towards the back of the house where a big barn with red siding had been converted into a design studio and office.

Hannah parked the car near a tall, magnificent willow tree. A petite, middle-aged woman approached them and introduced herself as Mr. Roye's Aunt Sue. She was Mr. Roye's right-hand woman and managing partner of his company.

When Ivy stepped out of the car, she looked so familiar that Aunt Sue was stunned. However, she didn't want to dwell on the feeling, so she quickly led the two ladies to the conference room on the second level of the barn.

The main floor was open concept, with a large fireplace across from the sliding doors, and the design studio, shipping and receiving area, and kitchen all in the same space.

The conference rooms upstairs had glass windows that overlooked the main floor. They were well-equipped with projectors and comfortable chairs. Mr. Roye's office was across the hall. Aunt Sue informed Ivy and Hannah that he was still on a conference call and would be with them shortly.

While they waited, Hannah carefully and neatly arranged the fabric swatches and folders on the table. Ivy was checking her presentation on her tablet. Both were confident that they could seal the deal today. This was a huge transaction; they couldn't afford to fail. Ivy smiled; this was the first product that she had designed, and she was pleased.

The conference room door opened, and Mr. Roye came in, apologizing for being late. His eyes lit up when he saw Ivy; he shook her hand.

"Good to see you again, Ms. Reynolds. As always, you look fantastic", Mr. Roye said while flirting

"Good to see you too, Mr. Roye. You're flattering me," Ivy replied, feeling uneasy but smile

"Call me Thomas or Tom, please," said Mr. Roye. Hannah noticed the way he seemed to glow when he looked at Ivy.

Aunt Sue invited everyone to take a seat. After chatting about their trip, Ivy and Hannah proceeded to talk business. Hannah gave the detailed presentation folder to Tom. Ivy proceeded with her presentation, showing Tom the fabric swatches that she had created with her suppliers in Turkey. The fabric was a combination of sheep's wool and cashmere from goats. The end product was the best choice for sweaters. It was light, comfortable, and warm.

They showed Tom samples of the fabric in twenty solid colours with five variegated options. Ivy then handed the sweater prototype to Tom; the sweater was a mix of yellow, light blue, and light green. The color combination was eye catching and gave off a positive energy.

"How fast can you produce ten thousand sweaters?" Tom asked. "And please try the sweater on so that I can get a good look at it." Ivy and Hannah looked at each other; did they hear Tom right? Ten thousand sweaters?

Hannah looked at Tom and asked, "Mr. Roye, ten thousand sweaters, right?" Tom gave her a grin and said, "Yes, ten thousand sweaters. I have 200 regular business owners that I am sure would be pleased to place an order as soon as I show the sweaters to them. Ten thousand will only give fifty sweaters to each store. This is equivalent to low inventory. So, if they want to re-order, how fast can you ship from the west coast? From the expressions on your faces, you must think I'm joking, right?" Tom laughed.

Ivy gathered herself. Tried the sweater on and showed it to Tom. When she had calmed down, she said, "Our production factory in Turkey makes 200 sweaters a day. We can produce your order in less than two months; shipping to us will take one month, then another two weeks to ship up north. The moment you sign the contract, I will email Sam, my business partner. She will place your order with our suppliers and personally select the best fabrics for your shipment. Your order will arrive by September for fall/winter distribution. I will instruct Sam to arrange productions of 5,000 additional sweaters to prepare for any re-orders." Ivy was ecstatic and so proud of her creation.

Ivy grabbed a water bottle and took a drink. She couldn't have imagined that this simple but elegant fabric would bring them bulk orders within just an hour of presenting it.

Ivy saw Aunt Sue smiling at their reactions. She proudly told Ivy in front of Tom that he acquired the business when he was thirty. He had managed to get lucky in trading. He had never thought of having a family, but these past few months Aunt Sue had noticed that her nephew was quite grumpy. She realized that most of his friends were getting married or becoming parents.

Aunt Sue was always reminding Tom to find a girl to marry. She told Ivy that he had even done some renovations to his main house, making it more feminine and cozier. Before it was more industrial looking; his kitchen appliances were made of stainless steel. Now he had added light blue-green backsplash. The living room had two big sofas facing each other and a big wooden coffee table with storage that he had found on his most recent trip to Thailand.

Ivy noticed Tom gazing at her as they listened intently to his Aunt. She smiled, thinking he must be pleased by her attentiveness. Eventually, Hannah pointed out that they should be heading back to the hotel. Tom stood up and offered to treat Ivy and Hannah to lunch. Aunt Sue was shocked; since when did her nephew provide meals to his suppliers? He hardly ever took her out for lunch. She asked Tom if he wanted her to make reservations and he nodded, then they all got into Aunt Sue's car and drove to the waterfront.

The waiter ushered them inside the restaurant and out to the patio. The atmosphere was homey; it was so comfortable and warm. While eating, Tom couldn't stop staring at Ivy's face; she was so simple yet sophisticated. She was pleasing to look at. Then his eyes saw the wedding and engagement rings, and he couldn't explain why it felt like someone had put a brick in his heart. He was thirty-seven years old this year; he had his fair share of relationships. But this was the first time that he had been smitten by a woman. She wasn't even his usual type; he usually preferred blondes.

Lunch passed without incident. Tom learned that Ivy and Hannah would fly back home tomorrow. He asked Ivy if she wanted to join him in Thailand for a trade show in September. Ivy said no due to her upcoming trip to Singapore. Tom said nothing but had an idea.

10

IVY AND HANNAH PACKED THEIR bags and got ready to go to the airport. Hannah settled their bills, then they returned their rental car and boarded the plane. They ordered champagne from the flight attendant and made a toast to a job well done. Good thing they travelled business class. Both were overjoyed and delighted because their business trip had been a success.

Ivy discussed all the important aspects of the contract with Hannah and instructed her to personally assist with quality control of the merchandise before it was shipped to Mr. Roye. Their flight was short, but they managed to iron out all the necessary details.

Hannah was grateful to be working with Ivy. She was a great boss, but Hannah didn't know anything about her private life. She knew that Ivy was married, and that she had a nice house. Hannah went there once when Ivy asked her to bring documents from the office when she was recuperating after her miscarriage. Hannah accepted the fact that her relationship with Ivy was employer-employee, and she didn't ask for more. Ivy was a considerate boss; she earned enough to sustain her lifestyle with the added benefit of frequent travel abroad.

When they got back to the west coast, the airport was crowded, and it was hot. Ivy took off her sweater; she had already sweat through the top underneath. She told Hannah to take the first cab home. When the next one arrived, she got inside and called Billy. He congratulated her on the success of her trip.

"See, when God closes a door he opens a window," Billy said. "Now you can get back to your old self and stop thinking about your ex-husband."

"He's not my ex-husband yet," Ivy said. "Remember, I still hasn't signed the papers. And why are you bringing that up when I'm telling you about the biggest success of my career?"

"Sorry, my fault," Billy said. "I'm just happy to hear your jolly voice and hoping you stay this way. The dark time has passed, and you need to find yourself again."

By that time, Ivy was only a block away from home. She said goodbye to Billy when the taxi stopped in front of her house. Ivy collected her things and put her cell phone inside her bag. She got a surprise when she opened the car door.

Vins was sitting at her front lawn. He was hugging his knees and seemed to be cradling himself. Ivy was scared and confused. She got back to her senses when the taxi driver asked her to pay the fare. After paying, she got out and grabbed her luggage from the driver. When she closed the car door, Vins looked up and saw his wife in front of him. He gave her a smile and was about to hold her hands when Ivy stepped back. She was puzzled, and she felt more heartbroken than before. Vins saw that his wife was unwilling to face him.

"Why did you change the passcode for the front gate? Do you want me to give up my share from this property?" Vins asked annoyed.

"Did you forget that my parents transferred our payment for your share after they paid our mortgage in full? This house is under my sole ownership now." Ivy reminded him, she was trying her best to stay calm. She smelled alcohol; Vins was drunk. She felt sorry for him; her heart melted, then she stepped forward to hold her husband's hands and asked, "Do you want to come inside? I could make something for your hangover?"

Vins held Ivy's hand and followed her to the front door. He wanted to give her a kiss, but he stopped himself. He still had mixed emotions towards her; he despised her, but he missed her at the same time. Ivy went straight to the kitchen and made some soup.

"Today is our sixth wedding anniversary. I wanted to see how you were doing after I left," Vins said.

Ivy felt that Vins was so unfair towards her. He hadn't once considered her feelings when he left her. Now he showed up at her house and wanted to see how she was doing after all this time? She wanted to shout at him, humiliate him, curse him. He had broken her heart into million pieces; she couldn't understand why it was impossible for her to hate him.

"Do you want me to say happy sixth wedding anniversary too?" Ivy asked Vins in her calmest voice while she stirred the soup. But deep inside, her heart was aching, and her mind was anything but calm.

The atmosphere inside their home had become awkward. Vins felt sober after hearing what Ivy said. *Am I insensitive?* Vins asked himself.

"Eat this while I take a shower. I had a long day and need to freshen up," Ivy said. Then she disappeared upstairs.

Once Vins was done with his soup, he put the dishes in the dishwasher and made tea for himself. He headed to the living room holding the cup of tea. He thought of following Ivy upstairs but decided to just listen to French music while lounging in the sofa. This home was so comfortable and inviting. The smell of this house was amazing. Why was it only now that he could appreciate this?

When he used to live here, he wanted to get out, but now he wanted to stay. He felt weird and indifferent towards himself. *What is wrong with me? Am I sick in the head?* He thought when he left his wife and moved to his rented townhouse near his wine bottle manufacturing plant that he was free at last. *Am I still in love with her?* When she was done showering, Ivy went downstairs to find Vins sleeping on the recliner facing the fireplace. She felt her heart flutter. She loved everything about this person sleeping in her living room. But she has no power to ask him to stay. She was afraid that he might push her away if she asked him to come back. They both needed to heal before starting a new life together if that was even still possible.

Ivy hoped that one day, Vins would return to her, and they could have a new beginning. She knelt beside him and stared at his gorgeous face. His lashes were longer than hers. But he was not sleeping peacefully.

Ivy wanted to check her email but decided to lie down on the sofa near Vins instead. This was the first time after their separation that he had come back; she wanted to savor every minute of it. After a while, she felt tired and closed her eyes. She fell asleep, and felt her husband touch her face.

She was awakened by her house phone ringing; it was three in the morning. She picked up the phone and said hello, but all she heard on the other end was breathing. After ten seconds, the caller hung up.

When she checked the caller ID she saw that the number was Vins's office landline. Ivy realized that Vins had left without even telling her. She felt betrayed once again. Was he teasing her, or was he just really insensitive? What was the purpose of showing up then leave without a warning? She tidied the living room before going upstairs and went back to sleep.

She was frustrated. Yesterday's flight was tiring, so she didn't wake up until ten o'clock the next morning. She had three missed calls from Hannah, who was in the office.

Ivy texted Hannah that she would be in that afternoon. She showered and put on her favorite crisp, white satin top and her navy-blue straight cut pants with a coat in a similar color. She wore her red satchel bag and red stiletto shoes and put on her diamond stud earrings along with her wedding ring and a watch.

She got her car keys and opened the garage door. When she sat in the driver seat and turned on the engine, she saw that she was out of gas. She had forgotten to stop at a gas station before her trip up north. Instead of getting mad at herself, she called a taxi to bring her to the office. When she arrived, Hannah rushed towards her, looking panicked.

"Our landlord sent an email saying that he won't renew our rental contract after it expires next month. He sold this building, and the new owner wants it to be vacated within three months."

Ivy grabbed Hannah's hands and told her to calm down.

"Please set a meeting with Samantha and Billy this afternoon to discuss our re-location," she said. In the afternoon, Billy arrived at the office and went straight to see Ivy. After exchanging pleasantries, they proceed to discuss their impending re-location. Sam joined them via video call.

Ivy asked Billy and Sam what they thought about purchasing a warehouse to convert to offices. She had gotten the idea from Mr. Roye's barn. It was cheaper to buy a warehouse than an office, based on the current market. Ivy presented the pros and cons of buying a warehouse. She explained it well, and true to her personality, Sam immediately agreed. Billy was a bit more skeptical, so Ivy showed him the cost of a mortgage versus an office unit at the current rates. She explained that in a warehouse, they could have both their offices and space for merchandise. In two months, ten thousand sweaters would be arriving. Ivy felt that they needed to think big this time. They would be able to put Mr. Roye's down payment towards the mortgage. When they had all agreed, Hannah contacted Drew, Ivy's realtor, and made an appointment to meet with him the following morning at ten a.m.

Billy invited Ivy for snacks at their favourite café. He said it was his treat for closing the contract with Mr. Roye and for buying their first property together. He was so happy that they would finally have something that belonged to them.

The atmosphere inside the café was lively, with friends chatting and bantering. Ivy and Billy bumped into some familiar faces and some even sat with them for a while. Ivy felt that this was like the old days. She wanted to tell Billy about Vins coming over last night, but she didn't want to ruin their time together. Because of work and kids, they rarely got to spend quality time together.

The next day, Ivy parked her car at the office, and let Billy drove them to the realtor's office who happened to be the same realtor who sold the lake house to Vins. When they reached Drew and Eve's office, their secretary ushered Ivy and Billy into the conference room and offered them beverages and snacks. At ten a.m. sharp, Drew and Eve entered the room and shook hands with Ivy and Billy.

Ivy's company was looking for a twenty thousand to twenty-five thousand square foot warehouse that could be converted into an office. They were willing to go uptown, maybe twenty to thirty minutes from downtown. Drew checked their inventory and narrowed the list down to a few available properties.

Billy saw the first photo that Drew showed them and fell in love with the façade of the warehouse. It looked like a home, with two dormers in front. The front door was on the right side of the building. There was an existing office area on the upper level. It was open concept; only the conference room was enclosed with a glass door and partitions. Ivy could picture herself working in the warehouse. It would cost them half a million dollars to purchase the space and around one hundred thousand to make it their own. They would have a pantry and an additional washroom downstairs.

Currently, they employed around ten people. Management would stay on the upper floor and the rest would be stationed downstairs. Ivy looked at Billy as if to say, *This is it! We have our office in a warehouse setting.* They both smiled and nodded in agreement.

Hannah asked Drew and Eve when they could visit the property. When all was settled, they finished their snacks and chatted. Billy excused himself to go to the men's room. Out of the blue, Eve asked Ivy if the Lakehouse on Pearwood Lane was to her liking.

Ivy choked on her coffee; she didn't know how to react. Her body stiffened and she broke out in a cold sweat. She gazed at Eve, feeling at a loss for words.

Sensing that she made a mistake, Eve said, "Vins gave you the lake house he bought last year for your fifth wedding anniversary, right?"

Ivy was numb and had no idea how to reply. Her face was pale when Billy came in. He was worried; he grabbed her hands and asked her what happened, but she didn't answer. Drew told Eve to stop asking. The room felt awkward, and nobody said anything. Most people still didn't know that Ivy and Vins had separated; Ivy knew that Eve hadn't intentionally ruined their meeting.

Hannah was fast to change the subject, telling Drew and Eve that she would wait for their call about viewing the property. She could tell that Ivy was distressed and wanted to get her out of that office as soon as possible.

Ivy tried to compose herself but hearing about the lake house had been a total shock. Vins had never said a word about it. She felt like she was being betrayed over and over again.

Eve apologized; Ivy brushed it off, explaining that she had forgotten about the lake house. They said goodbye; Hannah drove Billy's car and Billy sat in the back with Ivy, holding her hands. He wanted to ask her what had happened, but he decided to give her space. Even Hannah felt strange seeing her boss so upset; she was used to the bubbly, happy Ivy who never showed weakness and was always there to lend a helping hand.

Searching for her own happiness was Ivy's top priority after her separation from Vins. But today's incident was a big blow to her mind and body. How could she find her own happiness if she was still so affected by memories of Vins? She has so many unanswered questions.

Ivy had always given the benefit of the doubt to everyone. She had done her best to understand Vins all these years. How could he have done this to her? Never in her wildest dreams would she have thought that Vins could be so unpredictable. He has always been firm in his decision-making, never changing his mind and acting with honour and dignity. As far as she knew, she had been his whole world. She was starting to feel helpless. She had never doubted herself like this before, always telling herself that she would pick herself up whenever she fell.

Even when she was younger, she had never been bullied or tormented by anyone. She was always fair and open-minded, never judging a person by their race, occupation, or status. People had their own strengths and weaknesses, and people needed to support each other in order to make the world a happy place.

But now she felt powerless. Her mind was hollow, and her body felt fragile enough to break at any moment. She wanted to stay alive in a midst of sorrow. Giving up her relationship with her husband had never been an option. Every relationship was supposed to be a two-way street. She had no idea which way theirs was going.

11

ONE WEEK AFTER THEY SIGNED the purchase agreement for their new office, Billy contacted his contractor so that they could start immediately on the new design. The renovation would take one month to complete; thankfully, their current landlord was willing to grant them an extra month on the old lease. Ivy wanted to cancel her Singapore trip to lend a hand with the relocation, but Sam insisted she go. Ivy needed a vacation badly.

In her heart, she was ready to ask Vins about the lake house. At first, she wanted to just ignore it and move on, but she knew in her heart that she wanted an answer. She did her best to mentally prepare before talking to him. Sam and Billy learned about the lake house, waited to hear the outcome of the conversation.

The following weekend, she called Vins and arranged a time to meet. She suggested that they meet away from their former home and on neutral ground, somewhere that she could think clearly and rationally. Vins offered an address; it was the lake house on Pearwood Lane. Ivy wondered if she was really ready to hear the truth about the house, and if she would be able to accept Vins's reasons for keeping it a secret. So many negative thoughts were swirling around in her brain; she couldn't fathom what Vins had been thinking.

Before the meeting, Ivy called Billy and told him where she was going. He asked if she wanted him to join her, but she declined, telling him she would text him after she had talked with Vins.

When she pulled up to the house on Pearwood Lane, Ivy's mouth fell open in awe. This was her dream lake house that she had described to Vins when they were dating. Now it was real; she was staring right in front of it.

She got off her car and slowly walked towards the front gate, feeling a mix of emotions. The disappointment she had felt the first time she heard about the lake house vanished. Seeing the white picket fence, she had imagined since childhood, she felt as if she had been brought back to life.

When she came back to her senses, she reminded herself that the house didn't belong to her.

Vins walked out the front door and approached Ivy. He gave her a peck on the cheek and said, "Welcome home!"

Puzzled, Ivy said thank you. Vins held his wife's hand, and they walked the pathway that led to the back of the lake house. Then, to Ivy's surprise, she saw that the backyard was decorated with her favorite colourful lanterns, and there were six colourful Adirondack chairs ten meters away from the lake.

This is picture perfect. I'm living in my childhood dream right now, Ivy thought, her genuine smile visible on her face. But her eyes betrayed her true emotions; she could feel joy and ecstasy, but inside, she was shattered.

Ivy took both of Vins's hands in her own and held them tightly. "What are you doing to my heart?" she asked. "I feel like I'm going crazy!"

Without thinking, Vins blurted out, "I couldn't picture you in this house, Ivy."

He sounded arrogant and his face showed no emotion. He was still holding her hands.

"Why did you ask me to meet you here if you don't see me in this place?" Ivy asked. As usual, her voice was calm, but her heart was pounding hard. She wanted to punch Vins, but her love for him was still greater than her desire to hurt him.

"I was devastated when you left me, but I couldn't stay mad at you because I love you more than my life, Vins. I never asked you why you wanted to leave me; I gave you time and space for you to sort things out your way. I tried my best to understand you and to heal myself. Please be fair, Vins; you knew that I am hurting too. I know you must have had your reasons to not tell me about this lake house, which is beautiful, by the way. But if you do not want me to be here, why did you invite me over? Do you want me to feel sorry for myself? Do you really hate me that much?"

Ivy didn't know what else to say. She was struggling to breathe and sat down in a green lawn chair. This was like a roller coaster ride of emotions. She wanted to give up, but her heart was telling her otherwise.

Vins was emotionless when Ivy let go of his hands. He was speechless. He had no idea how to explain his decisions to her. He wanted her to stay, but at the same time, he wanted her to get out.

Finally, after what felt like a million years of silence, Ivy spoke.

"Is it true that this house was a wedding anniversary gift for me?"

"Yes and no", replied Vins, not looking at Ivy. He gazed at the water in front of them.

Then, something snapped inside his head.

He pulled Ivy from the lawn chair and dragged her towards the house. Her wrists hurt where Vins was gripping them. She wanted to get away, but Vins kept dragging her, almost causing her to trip. Ivy was too afraid to try any harder to escape.

When they got into the house, Vins pushed Ivy onto the kitchen island. Ivy looked at her husband; it was like looking into the devil's eyes. He was red and fierce and looked like he might be about to devour her alive.

Vins's hands were shaking. Without warning, he punched Ivy's left thigh. She screamed in pain and fell onto the floor. Vins kicked her and pulled her hair to make her stand then hit her in the stomach.

He hit her nonstop until his knuckles were bleeding. Ivy fell to the floor again; she wanted to shout at Vins, but she was afraid to agitate him even more. She fought the urge to scream at him.

By the time Vins stopped hitting her, Ivy was black and blue. Her left thigh was swollen, and she wanted to throw up. Vins had been careful not to hit her anywhere that would be visible while she was clothed.

Ivy hadn't cried while Vins was beating her; this made him mad all over again. He wanted to be in control, but Ivy was too stubborn to show her weakness. Did she think she was better than him?

Ivy was too weak to stand. She tried to stay conscious and not faint from the pain. She gathered all her strength and pulled herself up onto a chair. Still in dazed, she closed her eyes and tried to think of a way out.

She was waiting for a chance to call or text Billy, but Vins hadn't taken his eyes off her. He wanted to hear her beg; he thought she was an awful and vicious person. It seemed like he was about to hit her again when suddenly, his demeanour changed.

"What happened?" he asked her. "Why are you in pain?"

Ivy was shocked. She wanted to curse at him, but when she looked at him, his face was confused, pale, and blank. She realized that this was her chance to escape, so she grabbed her purse and ran, limping as she went. She had to get out of that place.

Ivy had thought that coming to the lake house would get her some answers. What she got instead was physical torture from someone who she really loved. She couldn't understand what she felt towards her husband. In her heart, she pitied him.

She decided to drive to the emergency room to get herself checked. When she got to the hospital, she told the admitting nurse that she had been physically assaulted but that she didn't want to press charges. However, the doctor insisted that they report the incident because of the seriousness of her injuries.

To pacify the medical personnel, Ivy agreed to meet with a female police officer. She told the officer about her visit to her husband's home and what had happened. Ivy said she wanted to keep the incident private and that she didn't want Vins to be arrested. The female police officer had no choice but to agree with Ivy's request. A police report would be submitted to the police station, but no further investigation would take place. She asked Ivy if she wanted to request a restraining order.

"Not for the time being," Ivy replied. She knew that she wasn't thinking straight and that she might regret it later if she made an impulsive decision.

Back at the lake house, Vins was still standing near the front door. He had a headache. He was shocked to see that his knuckles were bleeding, and his arm was in pain. His heart was beating faster than usual, and he was afraid that he might be having a heart attack.

He went to the kitchen and grabbed the first aid kit. He washed his hand before applying ointment to his knuckles and putting on a bandage. He cleaned the kitchen and fixed the chair that Ivy had accidentally knocked down.

The last thing he could remember was his wife's pained face. When she left, she had been clasping her stomach and struggling to walk. He wanted to remember what had happened, but his head was spinning. He decided to call Ivy to find out if she was okay.

He dialled her number and heard her ringtone coming from under the kitchen table. He picked up the phone and decided to bring it to Ivy at her house.

However, Ivy hadn't gone home; after she left the hospital, she had checked into a hotel about thirty minutes from her house. She decided to stay for one night in order to evaluate her relationship with Vins and recuperate from her injuries. Good thing she always kept an overnight bag in her trunk, in case of emergencies.

When she got to her room, she ordered room service: quinoa shrimp salad and hot milk. Not an ideal combination, but that's what she wanted. She told the hotel staff to deliver her food after an hour, so she could take a bath and apply medicine to her thigh.

After dinner, she wanted to call Billy and Sam to tell them where she was, but she couldn't find her phone. Luckily, she had memorized her office number and called there, even though it was after office hours.

"Hello, Top Fashion Atelier, Hannah speaking."

"Hey Hannah, working overtime? Can you give me Billy and Sam's cell numbers? I lost my phone earlier in an accident, but don't worry; I'm fine," Ivy said

"Boss, where are you? Sam asked me to wait here for your call. She and Billy have been trying to call you all afternoon. Sam sensed something was wrong," Hannah said, sounding worried.

12

WHEN IVY GOT BILLY AND Sam's numbers, she told Hannah she was free to go home, but asked her to buy a new cell phone for her to pick up on Monday. She wasn't worried because she had backups of all of her data and contacts that she would be able to transfer to the new phone.

Billy was calm when Ivy told him what had happened with Vins; Sam, on the other hand, exploded. She was fuming as Ivy told her about the domestic violence that she had suffered. Sam told Ivy that she had made the right decision in going to the hospital while chiding her for not pressing charges. Sam was furious and talked non-stop; Ivy could only sit back and listen to her rant.

When she hung up, Ivy finally had a quiet moment. She dried her hair and re-heated her milk. Her whole body was aching, especially her thighs and stomach. She would be black and blue tomorrow for sure. She prayed hard, asking God for the strength to deal with Vins. Was this a sign that she would finally have the courage to sign the divorce papers?

Without asking Ivy for permission, Billy called her parents and told Mommy Nas all the details of what Vins had done. He felt that he couldn't just ignore the incident; this was the first time Vins had ever physically harmed Ivy, as far as he knew.

Mommy Nas didn't say anything; she just listened, though her heart was suffering. Daddy Todd had been so devastated when Vins left Ivy that he had thought about hiring someone to hurt Vins. But because he and his wife were good people they had chosen to keep quiet and let Ivy deal with her own problems.

As for Ethan, Mommy Nas felt that they couldn't tell him what had happened as he was in the midst of rigorous training for his international race in two months' time. It would be unfair to let him know now and upset him. Mommy Nas decided that they would tell Ethan when they got to Singapore.

Mommy Nas loved her children unconditionally. She never nagged them; she gave them wings and the freedom to choose their own destiny. She believed that trials and tribulations were necessary in order to appreciate good fortune. She never shielded her children from pain, but she encouraged them to discover their own will to survive.

Ivy's misery should not be Ethan's pain. They were bonded, but they must live their own lives. They were family but they still needed to face their own fates. Mommy Nas prayed that her daughter would find peace and an end to her troubles. As parents, they could only give moral support and sometimes financial aid. After talking to Billy, Mommy Nas went to the kitchen and got a glass of water then went to their bedroom.

Daddy Todd was sitting on the bed; his eyes looked worried. He gave Mommy Nas a hug when she approached him. They never said a word; they just held each other for a long time. Both were mentally drained. They lied down to get some sleep, planning to talk about Ivy's situation the next day when their emotions had settled. When Mommy Nas woke up, she could smell the sweet scent of freshly baked churros with chocolate syrup. This was her husband's comfort food. She sighed, knowing a long discussion with Daddy Todd was coming, and that he would not stop until he knew the truth.

Mommy Nas went to the washroom to freshen up and get dressed. She wore her favorite floral maxi dress with her hair down. She put on a headband and wore her diamond earrings. She was pleased that she was able to look so dignified under pressure.

Daddy Todd was wearing his blue apron, dusting confectioner's sugar on the baked churros. He liked sugar but he seldom used it to avoid being sick. But today he needed it to make him alert. He needed to be strong while sharing his thoughts about their daughter's marriage. For breakfast, he made sunny side up eggs, Eggs Benedict, and hot chocolate to go with his baked churros. His wife prepared oranges and strawberries with a drizzle of honey. They used their best China and crystal glasses.

They ate their breakfast with heavy hearts. It was hard to talk about their children's misfortune. But they had to face reality. After cleaning up, they went out to the patio with drinking water in hand. It was a warm day, and the sun was shining. It was a beautiful morning; still, they had to focus on their daughter's issues.

"I think we have to visit Ivy more often than usual, and we need to give her moral support," Daddy Todd said. "I know it is difficult to give her advice, but we must try harder to encourage her to stay happy even if her marriage has ended. I was eavesdropping on you last night; even if I didn't know who you were talking to, I knew there was something wrong with Ivy. Even if you're not saying it out loud, I know you're dying inside. So please, share your thoughts with me and don't be afraid of my reaction. I will do my best to listen and avoid saying anything stupid."

They had been married for thirty-six years; Mommy Nas's emotions were written all over her face, and her husband knew them all by heart. Without keeping anything secret, she told Daddy Todd everything that Billy had told her the night before.

Daddy Todd felt devastated. "Remember when Ivy first introduced us to Vins?" he said. "We both fell in love with him. Maybe it was his boyish looks, or the fact that he's such a mama's boy. He radiated a sense of security as he stood beside our daughter. We could see in his body language that he was madly in love. In our hearts, we thought they would be together forever. When we found out that he had proposed and was planning their wedding, we sensed trouble brewing. Vins exuded an evil aura, the way he was looking at Ivy then. Remember, Nas?" he said, shaking his head.

"He was such a handsome guy with a cunning grin. I remember feeling like he was too proud and had bad intentions. We didn't say anything because we saw that our little girl was so in love with him, and the wedding was her childhood dream. Did we make the wrong decision in allowing her to marry him?" Mommy Nas said.

Holding hands and staring at each other, Nas and Todd tried to be strong for their daughter. They felt they have to give their opinion about their daughter's marriage. They decided to drive to the city to comfort Ivy and settle everything for the sake of their only daughter's happiness.

The following day, they decided to pay Ivy a surprise visit. Mommy Nas drove the car and bought some fresh fruits along the way. Ivy loved cherries and plums. Daddy Todd asked to stop at a liquor store to pick up some dessert wine for pairing with the fruit. An hour passed and they stopped at the gas station to fill up the gas tank.

Mommy Nas thought about the first time she had seen Ivy's house, how she instantly fell in love with it. When she was younger, that house would also have been her dream home. Every time they visited Ivy, Mommy Nas always felt at home and wanted to stay longer. But she was apprehensive because of her son-in-law. She hid her feelings towards Vins for Ivy's sake.

They left the gas station, and her husband took the driver's seat. Mommy Nas enjoyed the gorgeous scenery. Tall trees on both sides of the road, big farm houses that were well maintained. There were farm animals roaming around the stables. In contrast, the buildings were tall, and traffic was tight when they reached the city.

When they finally arrived at Ivy's house, Daddy Todd pushed the remote control to open the garage door. They were shocked to see Vins's car inside the garage.

Ivy had checked out of her hotel around eleven that morning and gone straight to mass. Still feeling sore all over her body, she sat at the back of the church. After the mass, she went to the supermarket and bought supplies for the pantry. She wanted to bake calzones. At the supermarket, she got extra virgin olive oil, fresh basil, and all kinds of her favorite cheeses. The supermarket was her happy place. She laughed when she thought about it.

She was smiling while shopping. She spent an hour inside the store, and after paying the cashier, she pushed her grocery cart towards her car and put her groceries inside. She went to the coffee shop to grab some cold drinks before heading home.

While driving, she happened to see a summer dress for sale in the window of a boutique. She parked her car and went inside the store. The sales personnel greeted her when she entered. Ivy inquired about the dress in the window. It was the latest design, only one piece per size. The store owner had designed it.

Luckily, her size was still available. She bought the dress and decided that she would bring it to Singapore. The dress could be worn formally if she paired it with her favourite stilettos and jewelry, or she could wear it casually if she wore it with her branded sneakers. Double usage, she thought.

Ivy felt recharged and ignored her aching body. As she was about to pull up to her garage, she saw Vins's car was parked in front of the house. He was sitting inside it. When he saw her coming in from his rear-view mirror, he got out of the car and waited for Ivy to open the gate.

Ivy had never been so afraid in her life. Her body was shaking, and her hands were trembling. She wanted to scream; she was afraid Vins would hurt her again.

She wanted to call the police, but she didn't feel that she could. She slowed down a bit to compose herself. Her hands were still trembling when she reached the gate. She pushed the remote control and the gate opened. She parked her car inside the garage. She saw Vins get inside his car and drive into her garage. It took five minutes for Ivy to get out of the car, grab her stuff, and lock the car behind her. She walked towards the front door and used her thumb to unlock it.

Ignoring Vins, she walked inside; her husband was five feet away from her. She sensed he was hesitant to follow her. He looked nervous and uncomfortable. Ivy left the door ajar; she wanted to slam it in his face, but she chose to be civilized and give him the benefit of the doubt. She felt a migraine coming on; her head was in so much pain. She wanted desperately to deny that her husband had traumatized her.

"You left your phone at the lake house yesterday. I came here this morning to give it back to you and I've been waiting all day," Vins said. He was haggard and unshaven with untidy, wrinkled clothes. Ivy ignored him, continuing to unload her groceries.

Suddenly, Vins grabbed Ivy by the waist. She jolted when she felt his touch. Her heart melted as his familiar scent lingered in her nose. *The scent of my security*, she thought. Everything changed from then on.

Vins held her shoulders and turned her around to face him. Ivy couldn't control her emotions and started sobbing while looking at her husband. His face was so peaceful, unlike yesterday. This was the face she loved most. His eyes were full of reassurance, comfort, and security. This was her Vins, who she married six years ago. This was her home, in him alone.

As if nothing bad had happened the day before, they kissed and explored each other without inhibition. Ivy never wanted the moment to end. She had no will power to stop him.

Vins felt remorseful; he had missed intimacy with his wife, and then one thing led to another. They ended up in bed. Ivy had no idea when they stopped. Half awake, she felt Vins cleaning her body and putting on her nightdress. He was taking care of her just like before.

She remembered the time when she had complained she was unclean after they had sex, and he carried her to the bathtub and washed her. Then she fell into the abyss of sleepiness with a smile on her face.

Vins felt revitalized the next morning. He went down to the kitchen to brew some coffee and cook Italian sausage with eggs. He made toast and squeezed fresh orange juice into a pitcher. He loved the feeling of domesticity. He set up the table the way Ivy liked it. Vins was always attentive to the way his wife decorated their house. Being a designer was her best trait. Her priority was to make their home sparkly. Vins turned on his Bluetooth and paired it with their home speaker. The sound of morning jazz was echoing through their home. He lit scented candles and took a deep breath. He loved everything today.

Satisfied with what he'd done, he went upstairs and woke up his wife. Ivy was deeply asleep when he removed the duvet and saw her thigh that was still tender from his beating two days ago. He felt ashamed and annoyed while looking at the black and blue marks. Only when he kissed her on the lips did she finally wake up.

Feeling shy about her morning breath, she immediately avoided him, but Vins continue to tease her.

"Wash up and go downstairs and we'll eat breakfast together. I hope you like what I prepared for you." Vins carried her towards the bathroom while kissing her neck.

Ivy felt that she was in paradise. She felt like she was special, and her heart was overflowing with emotions. Hopefully it would not explode, she told herself while smiling. It was like she was sixteen all over again.

Vins was finally back home. After showering, Ivy brushed her teeth and hair. She wore a white tank top and pink shorts.

Vins was walking down the stairs when the front door opened; and Mommy Nas and Daddy Todd walked in. Seeing his in-laws scared him.

13

VINS SMILED AND WALKED TOWARDS them. He gave Mommy Nas a kiss on her cheek and hugged Daddy Todd. His in-laws did not say anything, but they acknowledged him. They went to the kitchen and put the fruits and the wine on the counter. Seeing that the dining table was still untouched, they glanced at each other as if to say, "We arrived at the wrong time."

Daddy Todd shook his head, a disapproving look on his face. Vins asked his in-laws to join them for breakfast; he prepared two sets of plates and cutlery. Then the doorbell rang.

Daddy Todd opened the front door; it was Mama Belle. She walked into the house with a gloomy and worried face. She hugged Vins's in-laws and whispered to Mommy Nas, "Thank you for calling me."

When Ivy heard the doorbell ring, she immediately ran downstairs and saw her parents and Mama Belle. She was scared because she was wearing shorts and she knew that her bruises were visible. It was too late to change, though; everyone had already seen her black and blue thighs. She went to each of her parents and Mama Belle, giving them a hug and a kiss in greeting.

Vins was clearly nervous. Ivy embraced her husband and told their parents to sit down and join them for a meal. To divert their attention from her injured thigh, she announced her business deal with her VIP client, Mr. Thomas Roye. She told them about his huge purchase order and her trip with Hannah to the north coast.

The parents keep glancing at each other; decided to listen to Ivy as if nothing unusual was happening. Mommy Nas kept her poker face on; she put toast on Ivy's plate while Mama Belle passed the egg platter to Vins. It was harder for Daddy Todd to hide his true feelings; he was mad as hell, but he had promised his wife that he would remain civilized, so he kept quiet. To anyone looking in from the outside, it looked like a normal family gathering.

Ivy was shocked when, as they were finishing their meal, Vins confessed what had happened. He admitted that he had made the mistake of physically harming his wife. He did not explain why he hurt her; he never gave them a reason. Ivy was expecting him to apologize in front of their parents, but he didn't.

Daddy Todd wanted to punch Vins for hurting his baby. He made a fist, but Mommy Nas saw, and she held his hand tightly. This was not the time to harm Vins, though that time might come later.

Mama Belle was so ashamed when she heard her son's confession. She wanted to reprimand him, scold him, or give him a beating, but Ivy stood up and embraced Vins. Vins reciprocated and held her tight. Seeing that Ivy was not mad, Mama Belle remained quiet.

"Where were you when the incident happened?" Daddy Todd asked, his voice breaking; it was clear that he was trying his best to stay calm and be sensible. Vins let go of Ivy, then held her hand.

"It was at our lake house on Pearwood Lane. It was supposed to be my anniversary gift to Ivy last year, but I never had the chance to tell her until yesterday. Honestly, I have no memory of hitting her," Vin confessed.

Daddy Todd was about to say something when Ivy cut him short and requested a private chat with both mothers.

The mothers nodded in agreement, then Ivy asked her dad if he could keep Vins company while they were chatting. Feeling helpless, Daddy Todd helped Vins clean the table and put all the dirty dishes into the dishwasher. Vins brought out the trash bags. Once the dining area was clean, they went to the living room to keep themselves busy.

They sat away from each other. Vins could feel that his father-in-law was just being polite; there was fury in Daddy Todd's eyes.

Ivy asked the moms to follow her to the study. She's desperately wanted to know if Vins had experienced some sort of traumatic incident that would cause him to black out and act violently, as he had the day before. She thought this might explain how his demeanour could change so suddenly and drastically.

"Mom, Mama Belle, you both know how much I love Vins; you could never doubt that I have good intentions when it comes to him. Right now, I feel like it's my life's purpose to save our marriage. During our courtship and up to last year, our relationship was great; then the unthinkable happened. Mama Belle, do you have any idea why Vins has become violent? He never laid a hand on me until recently. You can't imagine the look in his eyes when he dragged me from the backyard into the lake house; you wouldn't believe it was Vins. He was evil in the scariest way."

Ivy described the beating, showing them, her battered thigh. "After it was over, he asked me what had happened, as if he wasn't the one who had just hurt me. I was so confused. It was like the real Vins was back; he was speaking softly again, and he looked like he was in a daze. But I was still so afraid that I took my chance to escape into my car and get away."

Mommy Nas's heart was shattered while listening to her daughter. She wanted to scream and blamed Vins's mom, but she knew it wasn't her fault. She was praying that Ethan would never know what had happened to his sister. Knowing him, Ethan would want to kill Vins for what he had done. There was an awkward pause. "Vins grew up spoiled," Mama Belle said. "But he knew his limits. We always attended all his school activities and tournaments. My husband and I never missed any of Vins's milestones, and he was a confident little man. He was respectful and obedient; all our friends who had children wanted their kids to be like Vins. Until he saw how his dad died." Mama Belle stopped talking and started to cry. She hated talking about that time in Vins's life when he had experienced so much misery.

"I wanted to bring Vins to a psychiatrist or a psychologist during that time, but every time I suggested it, he stared at me as if he wanted to kill me. I got scared and dropped the subject right there and then. I only hoped that Vins would recover from his loss. He was with my husband when he died. Vins was a happy child and was always the life of the party until we buried my husband. Vins became quiet and wanted to stay isolated from everyone."

She dabbed at her eyes and went on. "I remember he had two friends who kept him sane during that time. I never met them; I have no idea if they still hang around. Those two people were like Sam and Billy to you, Ivy. Despite everything, Vins managed to keep up his studies, and he was at the top of his class. He focused his attention on school and enhanced his knowledge of glassmaking. That was his passion until he met you, Ivy. Vins never showed his emotions after his father died, but the moment he met you, he never stopped talking about you. Sometimes, I wanted to ignore his calls because of his never-ending stories about you.

"He even visited me at home just to tell me what you two were up to. I saw my boy was coming back to me because of you, Ivy. This beating is so strange, and I am deeply sorry that you experienced this pain because of my son. I tried my best, but there was nothing I could do for him back then after his dad died. All I could do was be a mom. I hope you understand me, Ivy," Mama Belle said.

"How can we help you, Ivy?" Mommy Nas asked. "Belle, can you talk to Vins about this issue? Maybe he will open up to you. I won't let your son hurt my daughter again," Mommy Nas continued with a firm voice. Mama Belle was so ashamed. All she could do was hug Ivy. "Please take care of yourself, my child," she said. Then she went back downstairs to see Vins.

Mommy Nas looked at Ivy's bruise. She felt rage inside that wanted to come out. Ivy told her mother that she had gone to the ER yesterday and reported the incident to the police, but she did not press charges. She wanted to tell her mom that she felt traumatized by what had happened to her, but she was scared to cause her too much pain. Mommy Nas told Ivy that they would stay over that night so that Ivy wouldn't have to be alone, which made Ivy happy. When they went downstairs, they saw Mama Belle, teary-eyed, talking to Vins in the family room. Daddy Todd was nowhere in sight.

Mommy Nas went to the kitchen to slice some fruits and make smoothies. Ivy thought Vins would stay after being intimate the night before, but after talking to her son, Mama Belle decided to bring him home with her. She wanted to give Ivy some space and let her spend time with her parents.

Vins was so embarrassed. It's been awhile since his last visit to his mother's house. He kissed his wife's forehead before leaving with Mama Belle. Ivy felt heartbroken again; she had expected a better outcome after last night's affair. Ivy wanted to hold her husband's hands, but she needed to let go for now.

14

"IVY, ENJOY YOUR VACATION. DON'T check your emails and put away your phone as soon as you get to Singapore. I heard they have the best spas in the world, so please book a massage. If there's an emergency, I will contact Mommy Nas." Billy rattled off instructions to Ivy as he drove her and her parents to the airport for their much-awaited vacation. Mommy Nas and Daddy Todd had to laugh, because they knew Ivy wouldn't listen to a word Billy was saying. Billy was as protective of Ivy as their son, Ethan.

"Don't worry, Billy, I have a full itinerary for her," Daddy Todd said. "We decided to stay in Singapore for two weeks." When Ivy heard two weeks, she opened her mouth to whine in protest, but her mother told her to quiet down and let Billy focus on driving. Feeling defeated, she gazed out the window at the highway. Billy saw Ivy's parents laughing quietly in the rear-view mirror. He knew that Ivy was an obedient child. He glanced at her, feeling sorry for her. She always did what her parents wanted, except when it came to Vins. She had wanted to bring Vins on the trip to Singapore, but Mama Belle said no, insisting she spend the time with her parents and brother.

Ivy thought Billy would drop them off at their gate, but to her surprise, he parked the car and got a trolley to help them with their luggage. On their way to the airline counter, Ivy caught sight of two familiar figures sitting at a coffee shop. It was Sam and Hannah. "What are you doing here?" Ivy asked.

"Don't worry," Sam said, giggling. "I've already approved your extra week of vacation. I brought Hannah with me for you to approve your pending workload. She has also rearranged all your appointments. Billy and I will cover for you." She winked at Ivy and hugged her. "I will miss you, but you need a break," she said. After they were checked in, Billy and Sam reminded her again to have fun and enjoy her family. This would be their first vacation as a family in a long time. Sam asked Ivy to bring her lucky coin to Ethan as a sign of her support. Hannah assured Ivy that they would take care of everything while she was away. She wanted her boss to get back to who she had been before her separation from Vins.

It was a sixteen-hour flight to Singapore, and they were thankful that Ethan had given them first-class tickets; they didn't know how they would have survived it otherwise.

Their in-flight experience was marvellous. One push of a button and a flight attendant was available to meet all of their needs. Even Mommy Nas, who was usually so serious, was smiling when the flight attendant ushered them to their assigned seats.

Upon tucking their bags and carry-on luggage into their private cabin, the flight attendant brought a tray with hot towels. Another flight attendant approached them with welcome drinks. After a while, another attendant brought them the menu for in-flight food and beverages. They could also request their preferred food from the in-flight chef.

Ivy enjoyed every minute of their stay in the first-class cabin. She thought they must be in the best seats on the plane; she couldn't believe it when she learned there were also full suites.

Ivy was looking forward to taking a shower thirty-five thousand feet in the air. She loved sitting in the comfortable airline seats that cradled her body. The privacy partition was essential for sleeping. The airline provided them with branded pajamas and slippers, and an expensive set of toiletries. She had done her fair share of flying, but this was her favourite experience by far.

After six hours on board, Ivy decided to check out the in-flight amenities. When she reached the first-class lounge, she was surprised to find two men in business suits enjoying a glass of wine at eight a.m. They invited Ivy to join them; she declined and excused herself. As she made her way to the showers, she heard one of the men say to the other, "She's beautiful but her eyes are lonely." Ivy wanted to say something but decided to ignore them and not let them ruin her day.

After showering and watching a movie, Ivy went to check on her parents. Their private space was adjacent to hers; they were sleeping peacefully next to each other. Ivy was delighted with her decision to join them on this trip. They looked calm and serene. She would not miss this for the world.

Ivy sat down in her own cabin and looked over the itinerary her dad had made. She saw that he had planned a visit to the Singapore Textile Industry. She knew that they had come a long way from being a modest manufacturer to one of the fastest growing textile markets in Asia. Might as well check it out while she was there.

They arrived in Singapore after four on-board meals and about five litres of coffee. Ivy felt hot and irritable, but she didn't show it; her parents had always told their children to just smile when things were hard.

Before exiting the terminal, they grabbed their luggage from the carousel. Daddy Todd approached a guy who was holding a placard with their names. His name was Wei, and he would be their private chauffeur and guide for the duration of their stay in Singapore.

Ethan had spent a ton on this vacation. Ivy was so excited, and Mommy Nas felt proud of Ethan's achievements. This was the first time she had experienced this kind of travel. She was frugal, always saving for her kids and retirement.

Wei drove them to the Downtown Core District where their hotel was located. Seeing that the family was settled at the back of the limousine, Wei called Marlon, Ethan's personal assistant and certified bodyguard. Marlon was six feet tall with a burly build. He had gradu-ated with a degree in Economics and had tried for a career as a race car driver, but he had become frustrated. Working for Ethan was the best thing for him; he couldn't envision himself working in an office.

When they arrived at the hotel, Ethan and Marlon joined them inside the limousine. Ethan sat beside his mom and hugged her. He kissed Ivy and Daddy Todd. "Change plans," he said. "I asked Marlon to book us a five-room villa. I want to spend time with you all in a house, rather than having to meet up in a hotel lobby." Ethan smiled at his family.

That night, Wei would show them the best hawkers in the area, and they would experience how locals lived in Singapore. Ethan planned to spend time with them the week before his race. After, he would fly home with his family and stay with them for ten days before heading to the next race in Malaysia. Before Singapore, he had raced in Italy. He had been waiting for this vacation with his family for the longest time.

After a week passed and they had taken about a million steps all over Singapore, the family decided to stay home and enjoy the villa for a couple days before Ethan's race. Marlon hired a housekeeper and cook; they tried authentic Malay, Singaporean, and even Chinese food. There was an abundance of seafood; they even had live crab. It was the first time Mommy Nas and Daddy Todd had seen live crabs; they loved the chili garlic crabs the cook made for them.

Mommy Nas wished she could bring the cook home with them; everyone laughed. Ethan felt so blessed to see his mom so happy and cheerful. It was new to him, but he didn't complain. It was different with his sister. She seemed spaced-out and only pretending to smile. Ethan desperately wanted to ask her what was going on, but he didn't want to spoil their vacation, and he had to compete the next day. He hated Vins. After they separated, his sister had lost so much weight and stopped smiling. He saw that she forced a smile in front of their parents, but when she turned away her face was cold and drained of colour. Ethan missed his little sister. Sometimes, he thought about retiring early to spend time with her. He wanted to see her back to her old self before he settled down. It wasn't convenient for him to be in a relationship right now because he couldn't be tied down. Ivy rarely asked him for help, but Ethan wanted to be free if she ever did ask. The last time she asked him for help was when she was establishing Top Fashion Atelier. He had given her a loan which she had paid back in full, plus interest.

After dinner when everyone was settled, Ethan asked Marlon to drive him to a hotel near the racetrack. He wanted to check on his crew and his car for tomorrow's competition. He was sure he would win the race. His team had come in second place after last month's competition in Italy, but he had still received a good paycheck. This time, he would show his family how his passion for cars had brought him to the world stage. Ivy would have an adrenaline rush when she saw him on the track; he loved to show off for his sister.

The race was underway when Mommy Nas got a phone call from Mama Belle. Mama Belle was concerned about Ivy. She wanted to take her shopping when she got home and buy her anything she wanted. She wanted to treat her daughter-in-law and make up for lost time. Mama Belle couldn't ignore the heartache her son had caused, and she thought that shopping might make up for it, at least a little.

Ivy glanced at her mom; she was nodding at whatever the person on the other line was saying. She was so calm and focused while her son competed. After a while, she ended the call as if nothing had happened. She only reacted when she looked at the monitor and saw her son move from the number three spot to number one with one lap to go. She was praying that Ethan would win. Daddy Todd was sweating and nervous, and he couldn't stay still in his seat. Finally, they heard the sound that signaled the end of the race. They were staring at the monitor when Ethan Dacker was proclaimed the winner. Mommy Nas and Daddy Todd stood up and jumped for joy. They told the people around them that Ethan was their son. Some people congratulated them. Ivy cried watching her brother. It was an epic win for Ethan. She was so worried earlier; she knew the other drivers would make it hard for Ethan to win. But now, her brother was proclaimed as the overall winner. He made his family proud.

Marlon helped them make their way through the crowd to Ethan. He was soaked with champagne.

After taking a shower, Ethan met his family and introduced them to his crew. Marlon told them about the victory party that would be happening tonight. Wei drove the family towards the villa, while Ethan stayed behind.

The team manager, Pierre, punched Ethan's back and gave him a tight hug, congratulating him for winning the race.

"You made us all proud, Dacker. Let us celebrate our win tonight and enjoy our victory."

Pierre introduced his brother, Paule, to Ethan. "My brother is your number one fan, he took a leave from his job just to watch you win. We will see you tonight."

"I have my parents and my sister with me tonight. You should join us for dinner," Ethan told Pierre and Paule. Paule shook his hand.

The celebration that night was a formal dinner. Ivy wore a black lace gown with straps and a halter neckline. It had an invisible zipper and the sheath silhouette fell straight from the bust, ending with an illusion hem. Mommy Nas wore a green lace organza gown with a V-neck and A-line, princess silhouette. It had three-quarter sleeves and a sweeping train.

"This is the perfect gown to celebrate my son's victory", Mommy Nas said, smiling. Daddy Todd wore a three-piece suit in dark green to match his wife's gown.

Ethan wore a black, three-piece suit to complement Ivy's gown. He couldn't remember the last time they had celebrated together as a family. He felt like a teenager again. He knew that during his teenage years, they had gone to so many parties with his parents. He cherished those moments with his family.

When they reached the hotel, Marlon opened the limousine door for the family. Ethan got out first, followed by Daddy Todd, Mommy Nas, and Ivy. Ivy linked arms with her brother and waited for their turn to enter the hotel.

The venue was huge and could accommodate a thousand guests. This would be the second victory party that Ivy had attended with her family. An usher greeted them and showed them to their assigned table near the stage. It was a formal gathering with a short program.

Ethan's crew would be the highlight of the party. Ethan wasn't a one man show, after all; he won because of the work of his brilliant crew. Dinner was served before the short program. While waiting for the other attendees to finish their meals, some guests roamed around the venue, saying hello to friends and acquaintances.

Someone patted Ivy on the shoulder. She was shocked to look behind her and see Mr. Roye with the two men in business suits from the flight. Ivy stood up and shook Mr. Roye's hand.

"Mr. Roye, how are you? I'm glad to see you at this event," Ivy said.

Ethan stared at Mr. Roye's companions.

"Pierre, Paule, do you know this man?" he asked. He looked angry; if looks could kill, Mr. Roye would be dead.

Pierre smirked and explained that Mr. Roye—or Tom to them—was their cousin from the north coast. "He is in Singapore for business but ran into legal trouble. Paule is a lawyer and a CPA, so he called him for help. When he learned we were also in Singapore, he decided to join us for the party."

Tom had no idea that he would bump into Ivy at the party, but he was overjoyed to see her. Ivy introduced Mr. Roye to her family; Tom asked them to call him by his first name. Ivy informed them that Tom was the VIP client that she had visited with Hannah. Their parents greeted Tom and thanked him for the huge purchase.

Ethan hated the way Tom was gawking at his sister. He wanted to tell Pierre to send Tom away from her. Then he realized he needed to introduce Pierre and Paule to his family.

Ivy had never met Ethan's team manager before. When Pierre shook her hands, she wanted to pull away. The handshake felt weird and annoying. She had a bad feeling about Pierre then Pierre introduce his brother Paule. Ivy felt a strange emotion while Paule was shaking her hand, it was a pleasant feeling. Ivy learned that their mother is Aunt Sue who happened to be Tom's business partner.

During dinner, Tom couldn't stay away from Ivy. Ivy entertained him, but she felt awful. She knew that staying away from him might jeopardize their business, so she pretended to listen and kept him company. When she noticed Ethan's disapproving look, she excused herself and went back to her family's table.

The celebration ended. The Dacker family were all proud of Ethan's championship win. Before they left the hotel, Ivy saw Tom from a distance, as if he was chasing her. Ethan saw him too and shoved his sister inside the limousine.

Tom didn't get to Ivy in time. From her seat, she looked back and saw him staring at their car. Ivy was so mad at herself for being nice to him. If it were not for their contract, she would never talk to him ever again. Ivy found it weird that her client would be too clingy, and the way he looked at her gave her goosebumps.

Ethan felt strange about Tom; he was insensitive. His sister was just being polite, but Tom acted as if Ivy was his possession.

15

ON THE DAY BEFORE THEIR departure, Wei was assigned to drive Ethan's parents to explore the other side of town, while Marlon went with Ethan and Ivy to the Textile Manufacturing Plant.

Ivy purchased lots of interesting fabrics for her clients back home. Ethan loved to see his sister working with passion; her face glowed every time she discovered a new fabric swatch. He realized that his sister's charm worked wonders for dealing with foreign suppliers. She was given a huge discount, and arrangements were made to ship her bulk orders abroad.

After their long day, Marlon made a reservation at one of the new resort hotels in town. It had a sky park that was only accessible to hotel guests, an infinity pool, gardens with hundreds of trees and plants, and a public observatory deck with 360-degree views of the Singapore skyline.

When Ivy and Ethan reached the hotel restaurant, they saw their parents sitting by the lounge, laughing at whatever Wei was telling them. Mommy Nas was having a blast, and Daddy Todd was clearly quite smitten by his wife.

The hostess showed the family to their table; Marlon and Wei excused themselves to allow the family to spend some time together.

Their dinner went well. They laughed as they all shared memories from their childhood days. Mommy Nas told Ethan how proud she was. Daddy Tood said thank you to his son for his achievements. Ivy couldn't stop her tears from falling; she was overwhelmed by all the good things that had happened. She excused herself and went to the powder room; Ethan stood up and pulled out his sister's chair. Daddy Todd stood up too and held his daughter's, elbow and smiling at her.

When Ivy was gone, Ethan's demeanour changed.

"Mom," he said. "Please tell me what's troubling you and dad. From the moment I saw you in the limo that first day I knew something was wrong. Please, don't sugar coat it. I'm going to be staying with Ivy for the next ten days and I want to know what's going on." His parents were ready to talk.

"Vins beat Ivy up two months ago," Mommy Nas said. "I wanted to tell you then, but I was worried you would be too distracted to prepare for your race. Before we all went home, we knew we needed to tell you tonight. Vins said he doesn't remember hitting her, that he just went blank. Ivy said it seemed like a demon was punching her. He left her thighs black and blue, and her stomach was swollen. She went to the hospital and spoke to a police officer, but she didn't want to press charges." Mommy Nas's hands were shaking.

Ethan was so furious that his face turned scarlet.

"That bastard," he said. They were the only words he could find. Then he realized Ivy was two tables away from them. He couldn't continue to rant and pretended nothing happened. Their dad pulled out the chair for Ivy when she returned to their table. "What did I miss?" Ivy asked. Her smile vanished when she saw the hatred on her brother's face.

Ivy held Ethan's hand. "Vins wasn't in his right mind when he did what he did to me," she said. "I know I shouldn't make excuses for him, but believe me, he was really sorry for what he did. I forgave him. Please do not allow that incident to ruin this beautiful family dinner. We are so proud of you Ethan." Ivy then squeezed her brother's hand and flashed him a charming smile.

Mommy Nas and Daddy Todd were upset, but they still couldn't help but laugh at the way Ivy sweet-talked her brother, as if she was still a ten-year-old girl.

For her part, Ivy reassured her family that she would save her marriage and would persuade Vins to seek a professional help when they got back home. Her heart ached every time her family thought poorly of her husband. She couldn't allow them to hate him. Vins was her life, and nobody could replace him in her heart. She gave them all a huge grin and told them to continue reminiscing about the past.

Ethan exhaled and looked at his sister. "We do not know anything about your marital problems, but always remember to tell us if you need help. You know that I can't tolerate people who harm you, especially your husband. I don't know about your living arrangements, but for God's sake Ivy, protect yourself." His tone was soft but strong. "We are family. Your pain is our pain, and your happiness will definitely be ours, too."

"Sweetheart," Mommy Nas said, "I know your marriage was not always a bed of roses; you love Vins, and we know that, but loving yourself is more important. Living with someone who is mentally troubled is difficult; but we'll support whatever decision you make. We're praying that you will be alright."

Listening to her family made her daydream about the happy moments she had shared with Vins.

After dinner, the family decided to walk along the waterfront and enjoy the beautiful view of the city. Singapore was beautiful at night. A couple recognized Ethan and asked him if they could take a photo of him and "his beautiful girlfriend." Ivy and Ethan laughed.

"My sister is beautiful indeed, but I'm single," he said, winking at the couple.

The woman giggled and rushed to Ethan's side. She held his arm then instructed her husband to take the photo immediately. Their parents backed off a little bit and Ivy followed suit. Then the husband asked Ethan to pose with his sister. Ivy refused at first, but Ethan grabbed her, and they both smiled for the photo. The couple bowed and thanked the family, wishing Ethan good luck with his future races.

A crowd had started to gather, with more people asking Ethan for autographs and photos. He indulged them but had to leave before too long to avoid more people crowding them. He called Marlon to pick them up in front of the hotel. They excused themselves from the fans. Seeing his son being mobbed made Daddy Todd proud. Mommy Nas was annoyed by the lack of privacy but was still proud of her son.

Ivy was exhausted and had to stop to rest. Ethan realized that his sister was worn out, so he offered her a piggy-back ride; the hotel was only a short walk away. Daddy Todd helped his daughter onto on his son's back, remembering the times when they were little and would do the same.

Ethan had always been a sweet big brother. Their parents couldn't ask for more. Ethan and Ivy both laughed as he carried her towards the hotel; he teased her and pretended to struggle.

Marlon did a double take when he saw Ethan carrying his sister on his back. His boss was usually serious and dull when talking to women. He didn't give most women a second date; he usually found them too clingy, pretentious, or provocative. These last two weeks, Marlon had seen a whole different side of his boss. He knew he had to respect Ethan's family, and not to offend them especially his sister.

Ivy was beautiful, and her personality defined her. She exuded an angelic aura; everyone fell in love with her the moment they met her. Marlon was aware that she was married, though he had never met her husband. Ethan didn't say much about his family, though Marlon had overheard Ivy talking about the gift she had gotten for her husband.

Ethan put Ivy down when they got to the car in front of the hotel. She stood on her tip toes and gave Ethan a peck on the cheek, thanking him. Marlon held the door open for the family. They were all tired and quiet on the way home. Ivy sat between her parents. She leaned her head on her dad's shoulder and closed her eyes.

Daddy Todd was all smiles; he felt that his baby still needed him. Mommy Nas held her daughter's hand, wishing that she could be whole again and strong enough to face her husband's demons. Ivy deserved a happy and comfortable life. She would need to be tough if she was going to stay with Vins. Marriage was a roller coaster ride with lots of hurdles along the way, but love was love, no matter what.

The next morning after they had thoroughly thanked and praised the cook for her service, Daddy Todd called the housekeeper, Wei, and

Marlon to join the family at the dining table. He gave them his excess Singaporean dollars. He also told Ethan to pay them extra for a job well done. The family was happy with their services and ready to head back home.

The night before, the housekeeper had helped Ivy pack her bags, including some extra luggage she had purchased; she had so many things to bring home for her office and clients. It took them three hours to finish packing. Ivy gave the housekeeper a pair of European sunglasses as a thank you gift. Her parents had bought themselves a few things for their home, as well as a nice floral vase for Mama Belle.

Wei helped them load their luggage into the van; he felt sad that they were leaving. He told them to reach out if they ever visited Singapore again. After loading the bags and checking that his passengers were buckled up, Wei took the driver's seat. The housekeeper and the cook waved goodbye to the family as they drove away.

Ethan and Ivy sat beside each other on the plane; they talked about their plans for his visit. Ivy wanted to throw him a party. Ethan asked if Vins would be there; he needed to prepare himself to face Ivy's husband. Ivy asked Ethan to be nice and let her handle the situation with Vins.

They were surprised to see that Thomas Roye was once again joining them on their flight, along with Pierre and Paule. The three men were having drinks in the first class lounge. Ivy had mixed feelings whenever she caught her VIP client's eye. It wasn't possible for her to ignore them completely because of their professional relationship. But she couldn't stand his gaze, the way it seemed to get under her skin.

16

"ARE YOU AVOIDING ME, MS. Reynolds?" Tom asked. Ivy had just stepped out of the bathroom. He was waiting for her by the door, looking annoyed.

As far as Ivy was concerned, Tom was a client; nothing more, nothing less. They had no personal relationship. She had ignored his constant staring and extra attention and focused on their business transactions.

Tom, on the other hand, couldn't control his feelings for Ivy. He spent all night imagining her in his bed, even though he knew she was married. Her scent made him insane, and he wanted to cuddle her non-stop. He could tell that she had no idea of his desire for her. He wanted to tell her, but he didn't want to jeopardize their business relationship.

"Why do you think I'm avoiding you, Mr. Roye?" Ivy asked. She was beginning to feel irritated. "This was a family trip for me. As far as I knew, you and I had no business dealings to discuss. I apologize if I've caused you any trouble. If you'll excuse me, I'd like to get back to my seat. Enjoy your wine." She pushed passed him, pretending nothing had happened.

Ethan and her parents were settled in for the night. Ivy said her prayers and called the flight attendant to prepare her bed. "You're too stubborn, Tom," Paule said when Tom returned to his seat. "You were waiting outside the bathroom for her like a stalker; you came on way too strong." Pierre was embarrassed on Tom's behalf. "I just wanted to talk to her," Tom said. "I guess I shouldn't have asked that stupid question." He looked at Pierre and Paule, feeling ashamed.

Pierre held his glass and made a toast "To Tom, in the hope that he finds his own happy ending," Pierre said.

"I want her badly," Tom said. "I know she's married. But I like her so much."

Paule disliked people who wanted complicated lives. Tom had mentioned that he was interested in Ivy when they saw her at the party. Paule had reminded Tom to ignore his feelings and forget about her. Being a homewrecker was not a good thing. Pierre hoped that Ethan wouldn't find out about Tom's blunder. He knew Ethan's temper, and he didn't want to get caught in the middle.

Growing up, Tom had been a difficult child. He never listened to his parents, never followed the rules. During family reunions, he never failed to disappoint everyone around him. The only person he had ever feared was Paule. Paule was the eldest among the cousins and a straight-A student. He was also a wrestler; he was the family's gentle giant. He was soft-spoken but burly.

Tom's parents loved Paule and asked him to keep an eye on their son. He had graduated with a major in Finance then passed the bar to become a divorce attorney. The family could go to him whenever they had financial or legal concerns. Tom had become an entrepreneur because of Paule. He was the best financial consultant in their area.

After Tom's parents died due to an accident, Aunt Sue had stepped in to take care of Tom. She was so supportive and loved Tom just like he was her own child. Living with Aunt Sue's family, Tom learned how to share and compromise. Seeing that his cousins were diligent students, Tom was encouraged to study along with them. He ended up with a successful career, but he was lonely.

After breakfast on the plane the next morning, Ivy found herself thinking about Vins. She wanted to see him sooner rather than later. She was worried that he would be difficult to deal with when he found out that Ethan would be staying with her. She missed her husband desperately. They had been living apart for over a year now;

the last night they had spent together was so special to her. She hoped that their relationship had healed enough that he could come home.

At Ivy's house, her housekeeper was busy tidying up. Billy and the twins were outside in the gazebo. The twins were busy reading their books while Billy checked his work email. The housekeeper approached him.

"Mr. Vins is here. He's looking for you." The housekeeper didn't realize that Vins had followed her through the house and across the lawn. He appeared behind her and offered Billy his hand. The twins greeted their Uncle Vins.

"What time will Ivy and her family arrive today?" Vins asked Billy.

"Around five p.m., maybe," Billy replied.

"Can I go with you to pick them up?" Vins asked. "You can use your van for their luggage, and they can ride with me?"

Billy was stunned; he had no idea what was going on with Vins and Ivy's relationship, but seeing how eager Vins was, he agreed.

Meanwhile, Ivy texted Billy and asked him if he and his family wanted to spend the weekend at her house so that Ethan could get to know the twins. Billy felt sorry for Ivy because she didn't have children of her own; he was willing to share his twins with her. Billy called Sam and asked her to order food for Ivy and the family. They would welcome Ethan and congratulate him for winning the race. They were all proud of him. Billy forgot to tell Ivy that Vins was coming to the airport. When they exited the airport, Ivy was surprised to find two cars waiting for them. Ethan saw Vins first and wondered what he was doing there. He saw her sister's face glowing when she saw her husband. He looked at his parents waiting for an objection, but they said nothing.

Billy grabbed their luggage and put it in his trunk. Then Ethan patted Billy's shoulder and gave him a brotherly hug, taking the opportunity to quietly ask him why Vins had come to the airport. Billy told Ethan that he had no idea; Vins just popped up at Ivy's house and decided to come along.

Vins was on his way to grab Ivy's bag when a man he didn't recognize appeared out of nowhere and blocked his way. The man whispered something in Ivy's ear. He saw that his wife was caught off-guard; she was frozen and didn't know what to do.

Paule and Pierre had pulled Tom away from Ivy before Ethan realized what was happening.

Vins was shocked when he saw Tom. He couldn't believe what he was seeing, but he knew he would never forget that face. He was confused and had a hard time processing what he was seeing.

Vins looked from Tom to Ethan. He has been so sure that Ethan was the person he had been looking for all these years. The two men looked similar; they could be brothers. Vins was confused; he wanted to kill Tom, though he hadn't known of his existence until moments ago. His brain hurt and he couldn't think properly.

Ivy stepped forward and gave her husband a kiss on his lips. She held onto his right arm. She then introduced Vins to Tom, Pierre, and Paule. Vins's blood was boiling with anger. If it were not for Ivy holding his arm, he would have hit Tom by now.

Paule felt awkward about the whole situation and bid farewell to the family. Ethan told him that he and Pierre were invited to his victory party the following week.

"I'll email you the details soon. Pierre, bring your mom as well. Now, let's relax and recharge because in ten days we'll be flying to Malaysia to hopefully win another race!" Ethan smiled at the brothers.

Billy helped Mommy Nas and Daddy Todd into his vehicle alongside the twins. "We will go ahead, you and Ethan take Vins's car," he said to Ivy. "Sam will have dinner ready when we get to your place."

Ivy just nodded and said thank you. She had seen Ethan invite Pierre and Paule to the party; Paule had looked at her, and she was surprised to feel a sweet sting in her heart from his gaze. But she pushed that thought away and focused on Vins, who couldn't hide his anger from her. She knew he was jealous that Tom had whispered in her ear. She felt happy and in love again.

Vins looked at Ivy, hugged her, and kissed her lips. Ethan, Pierre, and Paule turned to look at them. Feeling awkward again, Pierre said his goodbyes to Ethan, telling him that he was thrilled about the party invitation and would ask his mother if she was free. Tom, on the other hand, was furious as he watched Vins kiss Ivy. He could see that they were a perfect match, and he couldn't deny the fact that they looked good together. Ivy looked at Vins like she was deeply in love with him. But Tom couldn't accept that Ivy would never be with him, not without a fight.

Paule sensed what Tom was thinking. He guided Tom towards the van that had arrived to pick them up, waving goodbye to Ethan and Ivy and trying to get Tom away as fast as he could. Tom would be in trouble otherwise. Pierre followed behind. The drive from the airport to Ivy's house was quiet; there was tension in the air between Vins and Ethan. When they arrived, Ivy was first in the front door. She headed for the kitchen, where Sam and Mommy Nas were preparing food. Daddy Todd went out to help with the luggage.

She was greeted by Brianna and the twins with hugs and kisses; it was clear they had missed their Mom Ivy. As everyone sat down to eat together, the children's laughter made the whole house feel alive. The conversation revolved around Ethan's victory, as well as Ivy's shopping spree for the company at the textile market. Ivy suggested that they bring the kids to Singapore someday. She wanted to share the joy of the place with her whole family.

Vins and Ivy couldn't stop holding hands under the table, like flirting teenagers. Mommy Nas was stunned to see Ivy so happy, considering how brutally Vins had treated her. Love was always love, no matter what happened in between.

In all the commotion, nobody realized that Sam was quieter than usual, and that she had a bruise on her left arm. Usually, she was loud with a high-pitched voice and sounded excited whenever she spoke. Tonight, was different. Only her daughter, Brianna had noticed the difference in her mother, and it made her afraid. She kept glancing at Sam, who noticed, and prayed her friends wouldn't pick up on it. She didn't want them to know what was going on.

She was facing a dilemma, and she wanted to hide from everyone until she had the answer. Sam wanted her life to be peaceful and successful, but the person who she thought would be her rock had destroyed her from the inside out. She told herself that she would protect her daughter in every way possible, but she had no way out. Her life was a mess, and she couldn't say anything because she feared for her life and her daughter's life. Sam had always been carefree and had dealt with her problems growing up with flying colours.

Her best friends always had her back. There was no problem that she couldn't solve with their help. They thought her life was easy-going and smooth sailing. They told her that she was the heart of their friendship. Sam was loud but she gave the best advise among the three of them. She was also an incredibly good listener. Billy could not survive without Sam. She was his go-to person every time he needed a babysitter in an emergency. Their company was doing well because of her attention to detail. She always completed people by being there for them, and she treasured all of her friends.

Sam knew that she couldn't hide her current situation from her best friends, but today was not the day to divulge everything. This was Ethan's special day. So, when the pasta needed a refill, she volunteered and went to the kitchen. The family looked at her without any suspicion whatsoever. Ethan thanked Sam. When she reached the kitchen counter, her tears started to flow. She felt so helpless and weak.

I need to tell them what I've been through all these years. I can't conceal my true emotions; I am sick and tired of pretending that I am alright. My life is a sham! Sam thought.

Before going back to the dining table, she went to the washroom and washed her face to help with the redness in her eyes. She collected herself and put a smile on her face, then walked in pretending that everything is alright. Brianna could tell that her mother had been crying.

She stood up from the kids' table and went to her mother, holding her waist so tightly that Sam jumped a little, laughing.

17

THE VAN REACHED PIERRE'S CONDO. Tom was about to get out, telling Pierre that he would stay with him tonight until his flight home tomorrow, but Paule pulled him back and did not allow him to leave the van.

"Do you think you can stay at his house knowing that Adelaide will kick you out the moment she sees you step inside?" Paule asked.

Tom scoffed and pulled his arm from Paule's clutches. "That woman never knows the difference between bantering and fighting. I just wrestled Pierre down, but I had no intention of hitting his head on the corner of the coffee table. It was an accident!" Tom complained.

"You never realized why Adelaide got mad? It was because Pierre went to the ER and needed five stitches in his head! The bleeding was so scary for her. Do you think she can forgive you that easily?" Paule asked. He told the driver to head to his townhouse and told Tom "Stay with me tonight and I will drive you back to the airport tomorrow."

The following day, Aunt Sue left the barn house office thirty minutes before Tom's plane landed. Having her nephew back from his business trip to Singapore made her happy, and she was excited to listen to his updates. Her two sons were living on the south coast, where her deceased husband's family lived. When she decided to relocate at the north coast after a terrible family setback, her children supported her and went with her. But after they graduated and had the opportunity to work on the south coast, they left her with Tom. Since then, she had seen Tom focus on his studies and eventually become her business partner. They had come a long way since that terrible day. Last night, she had reviewed Top Fashion Atelier's full delivery. The ten thousand sweaters had been delivered on time. Aunt Sue had delivered half of the inventory to their clients and was still sorting the other half before they could release it for dispatch. Ivy and company did an excellent job with the sweater fabrics. One of their regular clients wanted to order more, but Sue had told them to give her some time to sort it out.

After reporting to Tom, she was scheduled to check if the merchandising department could still accommodate re-orders. They couldn't afford to over-stock these kinds of sweaters. Tom's Singapore orders were for their spring collection that would be shipped by the end of December.

Tom waited for ten minutes before he saw Aunt Sue pull up in front of the airport. When she got out of the car, Tom was at awe when he saw she was wearing one of the sweaters that they had ordered from Ivy's company. She looked marvelous and young. The kaleidoscope of colors was perfect with her skin tone.

Tom realized that the colour combinations was complicated but had been properly executed by Ivy's team. Aunt Sue had paired the sweater with dark jeans and looked like a walking mannequin. This was a free advertisement. Tom couldn't stop admiring his aunt and in his heart he couldn't ignore that this was Ivy's perfect execution.

Ivy had miracle hands when she developed this product. Tom was looking forward to doing business with Ivy again.

"You look different, Tom!" Aunt Sue said as he put his luggage into the vehicle. He gave her a kiss and held her hands then examined her from head to foot.

"You look amazing, Aunt Sue," he replied with a wink.

"Hop in! There's snow in the forecast today so we should keep moving. I brought you your parka. It was below zero last night so bundle up!" Aunt Sue told her nephew while starting her truck and driving away from the airport. Tom put on the parka. He couldn't thank his aunt enough for always treating him as her own. She and his two cousins were the only family he knew.

"Aunt Sue, could you ask someone to grab me some bison burgers and poutine for my lunch, please? And can you take orders for yourself and the staff, too? It's my treat after my successful business trip. Then after their lunch, please prepare the conference room and gather all the department reports. I need to review them before we have our meeting at the end of the day."

When Tom was at the office, he never had to worry about time, being that he also lived on the property. This was a big advantage to working from home and owning a business—he always call the shots. No one could bother him and there was no traffic to consider.

He was concentrating on the department reports two hours later when he suddenly remembered the words he had whispered to Ivy at the airport: "Divorce him for me and I will make you happy!"

He couldn't explain why he had said that to her. The urge to let her know how he felt about her was too strong. He felt guilty when he saw her reaction; it was not what he had expected. Tom felt that Ivy was disgusted with him. And that bastard of a husband of hers just stood there, staring. To hell with Paule for pulling him away. *One day she will be mine, no matter what,* Tom thought.

Tom had had his fair share of women in his life, but Ivy is different; her love was worth fighting for. He sensed that she was doubtful about her marriage; her eyes said it all. They were gloomy and woeful. That girl needed to be cuddled and pampered. Tom knew that he could make her love him. He was very irresistible, or so he thought. A knock on his office door brought him back to reality.

"All the staff are in the conference room now. Are you ready for the meeting?" Aunt Sue asked. Tom had all the documents prepared. He knew that the meeting would be a success and that they would have an early Christmas break.

Three more months until winter. Their purchase orders were all delivered and ready for shipping. His employees were all dependable, and loyalty was always a key to a successful venture.

Since Ethan had been staying at Ivy's house for the past week, Vins hadn't visited her place. He kept himself busy with work and spent some time finding out who Thomas Roye was. He asked his close friend from the government agency to check Tom's background. He couldn't allow anyone to ruin his relationship with his wife. The way Tom gazed at Ivy was disturbing. Vins knew Ivy very well; she couldn't hide her facial expressions from him. Ivy had been disgusted when Tom whispered something into her ear.

Vins was desperate to asked Ivy about it, but he knew that he was not in the position to do so. He must work hard to gain Ivy's trust once again. His mood changed every time he called Ivy on the phone. He felt himself falling in love with her all over again.

One day, when they had met up for a lunch date, Ivy mentioned that she, Sam, and Billy were planning a party for Ethan before he left for Malaysia. She wanted to transform her backyard into a party zone, but she needed outdoor furniture to accommodate their guests. It would be an intimate, small gathering. Ethan had invited Pierre, his manager, along with Pierre's wife and mother. And Tom.

Hearing Tom's name made Vins irritable, and Ivy noticed the change in his mood. "Are you okay, Vins? You look cranky." Ivy said, hiding a mischievous smile.

"I hate how that guy looked at you at the airport. He clearly likes you, Ivy. Are you aware?" Vins asked. He had so many questions that he wanted to ask her.

"Are you talking about Mr. Roye? You're imagining things, Vins. He's just my VIP client from the north coast, and he isn't my type," Ivy told her husband while laughing and pouting her lips then drink her coffee. She took Vins's hand and squeezed it tight, reassuring him that she is not interested with Mr. Roye.

Vins continued to eat his quinoa salad and grilled salmon. They chatted for a whole hour. Vins realized that being with Ivy made him happy. Their separation didn't stop them from being in high spirits. Ivy couldn't control him, and he was free to do whatever he wanted. In his heart, he never had any intention to get back together with her. He smirked; he liked the way their relationship was progressing. "Do you want to use the lake house for Ethan's party?" he asked. Ivy's eyes widened.

"Are you serious?" she asked. "I love that house and I can imagine how we could transform it into a beautiful gathering place. You don't mind if we mess it up?" She was over the moon. She was delighted and glowing with glee. She imagined everything they could do to make the lake house into a place where they could have a party fit for a king.

Vins didn't reply straightaway, and his face went blank. Ivy was scared and stayed quiet. She remembered that look; she felt sick to her stomach when she recalled the ordeal she had gone through the last time she was at the lake house. The beating she had suffered couldn't be ignored. Blocking out her anger after that incident was the only way that she could move on; she loved Vins dearly. Now she was at loss again, confused why Vins's actions were so different from his words.

Vins's facial expression changed again. He noticed that Ivy had turned pale. Looking at her, his heart shattered. But at the same time, he knew he had succeeded in making her defeated and afraid. Playing with her emotions and making her suffer satisfied him. He wanted her to beg, but knowing Ivy, she never would. He wanted to strangle her; his goal was to be dominant.

Vins took her hand and said, "Feel free to use the lake house. I don't want other people at your house. That house is your private sanctuary. I would never allow others to gawk at you while you're living alone."

Ivy went back to her office satisfied after her lunch with Vins. She bumped into Hannah on the way in and asked her to bring a cup of coffee and some soda water to Sam's office. Sam was there, but she seemed different. Ivy realized that she had been acting strangely for several days now. She sat down on the couch and looked at her friend.

When they were younger, Sam never stayed quiet if she had a problem. She would always say that her problems would never leave, but she could. Then she would giggle until she had driven Ivy and Billy crazy.

Sam closed her laptop and looked at the goofy smile on Ivy's face.

"Why are you here with that stupid grin on your face? Did you get laid during your lunch date with your ex?" she asked. Then her smile fell, and she went back to her laptop, pretending to be busy. Ivy heard the sarcasm in Sam's voice and stared at her, trying to figure out what was wrong. She never meddled in her friends' lives; she always waited for them to come to her.

"He's not my ex, remember? I haven't signed the divorce papers yet," Ivy said. "And we have a change of venue for Ethan's party. Vins said we can use the lake house. We'll start at lunch and end at sunset. Vins invited you and your family to stay the night so that we can all stargaze by the lake. It will be fun! We can pretend we're on our annual fishing trip at the cabin. We haven't done that in five years. Whenever we're together and doing the things we love, those are the best times of my life. You know that, right, Sam?" Sam's face was blank and expressionless.

"We'll set up tents in the back yard and decorate the Adirondack chairs with colourful throws to make it festive. I'll light a fire in the fire pit because it will be cool at night now that it's autumn. Can you believe Christmas is in less than three months?" Ivy couldn't control her happiness as she talked to Sam about the party.

Sam got up from her desk and went to sit beside Ivy, holding her hand and leaning her head on Ivy's shoulder. "I miss the things we did together when we were single and free. It feels like a century ago, and my mind doesn't work well anymore. I want to spend more time with you guys. But you know, I have my priorities now. I don't want our friendship to suffer, but my family is my top priority now." Ivy patiently listened while Sam was talking. Reading between the lines, it seemed that Sam was hinting at a problem. "If you are ready, you can tell me what's wrong. You know that right, Sam?"

"Here's your coffee, boss." Hannah was at the door with the coffee and soda water. Sam jumped up and went back to her desk. Ivy took her coffee and passed the soda water to Sam.

Hannah told Ivy that she had gotten a call from Aunt Sue of Mr. Roye's office requesting a virtual meeting. They wanted to discuss next year's autumn-winter purchase order. Aunt Sue said that Mr. Roye had heard Ivy was developing a down jacket made in Asia, and he was interested.

Hannah waited for a response from Ivy; she thought her boss was daydreaming. Judging by the look on her face, she was in a happy place.

"Please call Aunt Sue and tell her that we're not ready to discuss anything yet, but the moment I finalize our down jacket I will be calling them personally. And please tell her thank you for their recent orders," Ivy told Hannah. With her boss's instructions, Hannah left.

Ivy and Sam resumed chatting about the party on Saturday. They had five days to prepare. Sam was in charge of ordering food, and Ivy was in charge of decorations and refreshments. They decided that Billy would set up the tents and handle the fire pit, as well as pick up the fishing gear. The lake in Vins's backyard was a trout haven. Ivy would tell Vins to clean his huge grill. Steak would definitely be on the menu.

18

IVY GOT ETHAN'S GUEST LIST. He had invited Pierre and his wife, along with Marlon and two other crew members. Pierre's mother and Tom would also be coming. Paule couldn't join them because he was on a business trip. Ivy was disappointed that Paule wouldn't be there, though she tried to ignore the feeling.

There would be fourteen people in total, not including the kids. Reviewing the guest list made Ivy smile and think about her wedding day.

This was the first party she had thrown for her brother. They had been bonding over the past week. They always ate dinner together, whether they dined out or cooked at home. After every meal, they sat by the gazebo and sipped their favourite wine. The days were getting shorter, and they both enjoyed the autumn weather; not too hot, not too cold. Ethan was enjoying his sister's company. She was always smiling and never unhappy.

Ivy's pantry and refrigerator were full of Ethan's favourite foods and beverages. Ethan transferred money to her account, but Ivy returned it. She told him he was free to stay anytime. Ethan helped his sister by keeping her house clean. He had grown up with Daddy Todd's guidance in the house clean. His mantra was, "When your woman is happy, your daily life will be peaceful and quiet." Ethan would never forget that.

Every time Ivy came home, her house was clutter-free. "You don't have to do that Ethan, I have a housekeeper. I can call her anytime to do this. You are here to relax and recharge," Ivy told her brother when she saw him with a feather duster in his hand.

"You know I got bored doing nothing," he said. "I'm staying here so will keep your house clean. Remember, I lived alone in Barcelona, so I'm used of doing chores. Did you bring me the Peri-Peri chicken I like?"

"Get dressed, I'll take you out for Peri-Peri chicken," Ivy said, laughing. "It will be freshly cooked, and we can have fries and cardamom rice on the side. I can order you a whole chicken so your craving will be satisfied."

"You're making me drool! Call Billy and Sam and ask them to come with us. The kids, too!" Ethan said, as he ran up the stairs to change.

Sam wasn't free but Billy and the kids were happy to join them. Ivy drove to the restaurant in her SUV. Ethan was always nervous when he was in the car with her, even though he knew she was an expert driver. She accelerated, laughing as he clutched his seatbelt for dear life.

"You may be a champion race car driver, but you're also a coward!" Ivy teased. "Don't fret, you trained me, remember? Never doubt your protégé; I will never harm you, my mentor!" Ivy's face was red, and her cheeks hurt from laughing.

"Ivy, stop messing around!" Ethan said. He couldn't explain why he was so nervous, even though he knew his sister was a good driver. He finally calmed down when they got to the restaurant. Billy and the kids were already at their table when they arrived. Ethan kissed the kids in greeting and Billy gave Ivy a hug.

"Let's order and then we can discuss what you'll be doing to help out with the party on Saturday," Ivy said to Billy while she looked at the menu. "By the way, we've changed the venue. It's at Vins's lake house now."

Ethan and Billy exchanged glances. The waiter came to take their order, then Ethan said, "Why are you inconveniencing Vins with this party? You know how I feel about him. This party is for me and my crew, it has nothing to do with Vins. What's going on with you two, anyway?" He looked at Billy. "Do you have a good relationship with him now, too?" he asked, frowning.

"He wanted to ride with me to the airport to pick Ivy up after Singapore," Billy said. "He seemed sincere, so I gave him the benefit of the doubt. I haven't spoken to him otherwise."

Ivy wasn't worried about her brother's concern. She explained that Vins had offered his house because it was more spacious, and because he didn't want people snooping on Ivy in her home. She was grinning because she felt so loved by her husband. "Mom Ivy, what can we do at Uncle Vins's lake house? Does he has a boat that we could use?" Lucas asked in between bites of French fry.

"I want to sit by the lake and watch the ducks and birds," Shelly said. Ivy told them that Uncle Vins had invited them to sleep over and see the stars. When the twins heard that, their eyes lit up and they nodded in unison. They had never been to a lake and had never experienced star gazing. It would be nature at its best.

Ivy also invited the kids to go on a shopping spree with her and their uncle Ethan the next day to pick up everything they would need for the party. They were both thrilled.

Dinner was a success; Ethan said he wanted to have another dinner there before he left for Malaysia, and he asked Ivy to buy a bottle of Peri-Peri sauce.

When they got home, the siblings were confused seeing lights on inside the house. Ivy asked Ethan if he had left the lights on. He said no, and that he had even double checked the house before locking the door earlier. Ethan was worried, thinking about what would happen to his sister if something like this happened after he was gone, and she was living alone.

However, when Ivy opened the gate they realized that it was just their parents' car in the driveway.

"Surprise!" Mommy Nas and Daddy Todd shouted in unison while pulling the string on a tube confetti. Ethan was surprised that his parents would do something like this, especially his usually strict and proper mother. Ivy gave them the thumbs up and said, "Good job, you two, you got him good!" Ethan was surprised to see his sister laughing. He had been waiting to see her laugh since the separation.

Ethan loved to see the change in his mom and sister. Daddy Todd was enjoying it too, bantering and joking with them both. Their trip had not gone to waste. Their parents were supposed to arrive the following day for the party, but Ivy had plotted with them to surprise him.

After taking showers, the siblings went downstairs for a night cap. Their parents had brought their favourite wine. Sitting at the main dining area, the family of four shared a drink or two. They are discussing what to expect from tomorrow's party at the lake house. Ivy said that with her two best friends assistance the party will be a blast.

It was the day of the party, and before the family headed out to the lake house, they went out for breakfast at the yacht club with one of Ethan's old friends.

After breakfast, Ivy got a call from Vins as they were walking back towards her car. "Where are you?" he asked. "I thought you would be at the lake house early?"

"I'm about to drive there, just that…" Ivy paused, and she thought his voice sounded accusing. She was annoyed; her day had already gotten off on the wrong foot. Ethan's friend had stared at her all through breakfast, making her uncomfortable. She was annoyed with Vins; she had never felt that way before the separation. She was disgusted and on the brink of shouting at her husband. She felt humiliated, as if she was being reprimanded for escaping him. Her attitude towards her husband was always loving, but it was different this time. She thought of blocking his number to stop him from harassing her.

Vins heard the irritation in Ivy's voice and immediately changed his tone. "Alright, drive safely and I'll see you in a while," he said. "No speeding, and follow the road signs, please."

Ivy hung up and got into her car. Her parents and brother were taking a separate vehicle, and she saw them pulling out of the parking lot. The night before, her parents hadn't responded when she told them she was planning to stay overnight at Vins's house after the party. They were aware that her best friends would be staying for the night, too. She felt that her family was ignoring her good relationship with her husband. Things became awkward every time the topic of Vins came up.

How can they reject him? she asked herself. Vins had only hit her once and she understood why he did it. In her mind, her husband was suffering from a mental breakdown caused by the trauma in his childhood. She wished her parents could be open-minded about her difficulties with her husband. Vins had dedicated his life to her, or so she thought. It was only her irritation towards the man at breakfast that had made her grumpy with Vins. She hadn't noticed that she was speeding, overtaking other drivers who honked at her in annoyance.

Ivy felt that her heart was beating faster than usual. She had no idea why she hated Ethan's friend. She could never have imagined that someone could be so conceited. Ivy knew that her brother had noticed how the guy was staring at her, but he didn't do anything to stop him. Even their mother could see how uncomfortable Ivy was.

The staff and caterer had arrived half an hour ago and were setting up the tables and chairs in the backyard facing the beautiful lake. Opposite the lake house was Mount Terren; it was magnificent, with trail hikes and crystal-clear water. It was a perfect view to wake up to while pondering the day to come and sipping a cup of hot coffee.

The lake house was everyone's dream home. Vins was immensely proud; the house was his prized possession, which he had once wanted to share with his wife. He heard a car in the driveway and, thinking it was Ivy, he made his way to the front yard. However, it was Sam and Brianna who had just arrived. He felt uncomfortable being around them without Ivy.

"Where the hell is she," he whispered to himself. Then he remembered that she had been driving to the lake house alone, and that she had been in a bad mood.

Sam patted Vins on the shoulder and thanked him for inviting them to spend the night at the house. He nodded, then showed her up to the room where she and Brianna would be staying. The room had a view of the lake and was one of three bedrooms upstairs.

The master bedroom was on the ground floor with its own sliding door facing the lake. Vins had added a terrace outside the room with a dining table and chairs. He had also added a fireplace. He drank his coffee there in the morning. During construction of this additional area, he had envisioned hosting a large gathering every summer. Now, it is a reality. In an hour or two, his home would be packed with family and friends.

19

ON THE WAY FROM BREAKFAST to the lake house, Daddy Todd looked in his rear-view mirror and noticed that Ivy was behind them. He felt at ease seeing his daughter. Mommy Nas and Ethan were chatting about what to expect from that day's celebration.

Sensing that something was wrong, Daddy Todd looked behind him again. He frowned when he saw that Ivy had her hazard lights on. Ethan noticed his father's unease; he turned around and watched as Ivy pulled into a gas station. Suddenly he was sweating and nervous; he felt that something was wrong with Ivy. She would never use her hazard lights unless it was an emergency. That was one of the first lessons he had ever taught her.

Ethan tried to calm himself down. He looked around and saw that there was an area ahead where his dad could make a U-turn. He pointed it out. He then tried to call Ivy, but she didn't pick up. Daddy Todd made the U-turn and within a couple minutes they were pulling into the gas station. Daddy Todd was praying that nothing had happened to his daughter.

The moment the car was parked, Ethan jumped out and ran to his sister. He could see that her face was resting on the steering wheel. He tried to open the door, but it was locked from the inside. He pounded on the window, but Ivy didn't move. He told his parents to call 911.

Then Ivy stirred and looked up. Her face was so pale that it seemed like no blood was flowing in her veins. When she saw Ethan, she opened the door. He grabbed her and hugged her tightly.

"What happened to you? Why do you look like a ghost? Are you okay? We need to bring you to the hospital."

"I'm not sure what happened, but I felt dizzy, and my eyes keep shutting. My stomach felt weird, too!" Ivy said.

The paramedics arrived immediately. They transported Ivy to the Regional Medical Centre. When they arrived, medical staff swept her away into the ER, leaving her family in the waiting room. She was nauseous; the doctor ordered a pregnancy test, though Ivy was in too much pain to notice.

Daddy Todd and Ethan went back to the gas station to collect Ivy's car, then Ethan drove it back to the medical center. When they returned, they saw Mommy Nas coming out of the ER with a huge smile on her face. Daddy Todd stood in front of his wife, looking confused.

"Did you win a lottery?" he asked sarcastically.

"Ivy is three months pregnant. We will be grandparents soon. Wonderful news, right? I am so happy that I cannot stop smiling," Mommy Nas told her husband.

Ethan was feeling mixed emotions and hit him hard. He couldn't imagine how his sister would manage to support a baby right now. Her bastard husband still hadn't accepted responsibility for his actions. Would they go back together, or would they continue to live separately? He couldn't focus; he was too worried about his sister. He paced back and forth through the ER hallway.

"Ethan, your phone is ringing, do you want to answer it?" Mommy Nas said. She was annoyed but still couldn't stop smiling.

She also had reservations about the news. If she was asked, she would advise her daughter to keep the baby and focus on her pregnancy. Ivy had had two previous miscarriages, and this might be her last chance at a pregnancy. She remembered how the last time, the doctor had told Ivy that her uterus was too thin, and she may never be able to conceive again.

But it had happened. Mommy Nas was over the moon; this baby would be so loved. It was six years ago that Ivy had gotten married. Better late than never for a grandchild.

It was Pierre who was calling Ethan, confirming directions to the lake house. They were on their way. Ethan told him that they had run into a situation, but that they would be there as soon as possible.

The door of the ER opened, and the nurse called for Ivy's family. They went inside and stayed at Ivy's bedside. Ivy told them to go to the lake house without her; Billy would pick her up in about an hour. To avoid suspicion, she told them to tell Vins that she and Billy had to run some errands for the company. Ivy would keep her pregnancy secret from Vins this time. She couldn't bear to lose this baby, and she was scared that Vins might hurt her again if he found out.

It was difficult to convince Mommy Nas to leave Ivy; Daddy Todd also wanted to stay. But Ethan told them that they should respect Ivy's wishes, as she might have a good reason for wanting some time to herself.

When the nurse told Ivy that her family left, she cried uncontrollably. She did not expect this, but she was glad that it had happened. Ivy was overjoyed and confused to be pregnant. When the nurse heard her crying, she discouraged Ivy for the sake of her unborn child. She reminded Ivy about the doctor's instructions that she must not stress herself, and that she needed to be careful during her pregnancy.

When Billy and the twins arrived at the Medical Center, Ivy was sitting in a wheel chair, still pale but she is glowing with happiness. Ivy waved, and the twins ran towards her with confused looks on their faces.

"Are you sick, Mom Ivy?" they asked. She reassured them that she was fine, and they both hugged her and held her hands.

Billy settled the twins in the waiting area and pushed Ivy's wheelchair to a more private spot. He wanted to get the details of what had happened. "What happened?" he asked.

Ivy told Billy about her morning, how she had been creeped out by Ethan's friend at breakfast and annoyed with Vins on the phone.

Then she had felt sick and dizzy in the car, and the next thing she knew, she was in the hospital.

"I'm three months pregnant. Can you believe it? We did it one time and boom, this happened." Ivy caressed her flat tummy with a huge smile on her face. She was mimicking Sam's way of speaking. Sharing her pregnancy with Billy was what she had wanted for the longest time. Ivy hid all her anxiety and fear about her pregnancy from Billy, pretending to be jolly while she told him about it.

"Are you serious? And why are you talking like Sam?" Billy asked with a doubtful voice and a grumpy face.

"Because every time Sam has a problem she uses this voice and her problem goes away," Ivy said, and realizing that the three men who knew about her pregnancy were all unhappy.

Billy saw that Ivy was irritated, so he tried to smile and congratulated her. Ivy told him that it was a secret, and he couldn't tell anyone, other than Sam.

When he heard that Ivy wasn't planning on telling Vins about the baby, Billy felt joy and sorrow all at once. He was once been kept in the dark about the twins. As a father, Vins still had the right to know about the pregnancy, regardless of what he had done.

When they reached the lake house, Billy parked his car inside the garage besides Vins's truck. He helped Ivy get out of the car and slowly guided her to the master bedroom. Ivy discussed with him earlier that she had to stay within the vicinity of the celebration.

When Vins saw Billy holding Ivy by the arm he felt jealous, so he walked towards them and asked Billy what happened.

"She sprained her left ankle, so she needs to walk slowly," Billy said.

Vins told Billy that he would assist Ivy to the master bedroom. Before Billy could answer, Ivy asked him if he could ask Ethan to grab her overnight bag from the back seat of her car. She wanted to shower and change her clothes. Vins stopped Billy and told him that he would get the car key from Ethan and get the bag.

When Ivy had her bag, Vins took Billy and the twins and showed them to their room. He told the kids where the fishing gear was, and that they could go find their Uncle Ethan to help them set everything up. The kids were so thrilled; Shelley hugged Vins, and even though he hated children, his heart softened a little.

Ivy was sitting in a chair on the master bedroom terrace overlooking the lake. She could see the gazebo decorated with hanging plants and colourful lights.

She could smell the food. Ethan's crew were having cocktails by the Adirondack chairs near the dock. The fire pit was lit, and the fishing rods were set up and ready for the kids.

Sam came down when she heard that Ivy and Billy had arrived. Brianna came with her, and the moment she saw the twins, she couldn't stop laughing. She wanted to show them the s'mores station that Uncle Ethan had requested for them. Uncle Ethan was the best, she said.

Ethan appeared and sat down beside Ivy, giving Brianna a kiss on the cheek. Vins felt awkward, so he told the kids he would show them the fishing gear.

After Vins left, Ethan, Sam, and Billy turned to Ivy, ready to listen to what would she had to say about the earlier incident. Before Ivy could speak, her parents joined them on the terrace as if they were having a meeting. All five of them were anxiously waiting for her explanation.

Ivy told them about the difficulty she was facing with the pregnancy because of her thin uterus. But she assured them that she was going to do everything possible to carry the baby to term, including getting plenty of rest and changing her diet. "I'm going to keep the baby," she said, "and hide the pregnancy from Vins until after the birth." She had finally accepted that Vins would have a problem with her pregnancy.

20

EVERYONE ELSE HAD LEFT THE terrace, but Ethan stayed behind with Ivy. Pierre came over and introduced his wife, Adelaide, to the siblings. Ivy extended her right hand to Adelaide while sitting down. Adelaide found that rude, so she ignored it and said hello to Ethan.

"Don't mind my sister," Ethan said. "She hurt her ankle so she can't stand up. Help yourself to whatever you want to eat or drink!"

Pierre told Ivy that she had a beautiful home. He saw Vins with the kids and found the atmosphere homey and family oriented.

As if he could sense that someone was talking about him, Vins turned around and saw Pierre and his wife talking to Ethan and Ivy. Vins didn't like it, so he told the kids to find their dad to help them. He was going to see his wife.

He stopped to get some food for her. When he looked up from the table, Vins saw that Tom and an older woman had joined in the conversation. He rushed to Ivy's side and put his hand on her shoulder. Ivy looked up at him, smiling.

"You need to eat, hon," he said, holding up a strawberry.

Ivy bit the strawberry from Vins's hand. Vins gently wiped his wife's face with a tissue. She then gave Vins a kiss.

Tom was disgusted by seeing Ivy kiss her husband; he felt that his blood vessels would explode with anger. He closed his fist as if he wanted to punch someone.

Adelaide told Pierre to get her some food; he knew what she liked. She wanted to chat with Ivy about the lake house. She wished to have a tour of the place if the couple didn't mind. Pierre looked at Vins and asked if it was alright for them to take a tour. Vins had anticipated that the guests would want tours, so he was willing to show them around.

By that time, Tom was walking to the gazebo followed by Aunt Sue and Ethan.

"My apologies to your husband, Ivy," Adelaide said once they were out of earshot. "That cousin of Pierre's couldn't stop gazing at you as if he wanted to swallow you alive. His smugness gets him in trouble all the time. Don't listen to his lies. The family gossip is that he made huge trouble for his relatives, forcing them to move. I have no idea what it was, but I think it has to do with someone being hurt because of his recklessness." Adelaide was sweating, which always happened when she got excited. "He was only a teenager when that incident occurred. Every time I ask Pierre about the details, he ignores me. He says that it's water under the bridge now." Adelaide couldn't stop talking. She was sweating so much that her makeup had started to smudge.

Ivy handed her a tissue and asked her if she needed to go to the washroom to freshen up. Adelaide declined; she wiped her face using the tissue Ivy had handed her.

Vins wanted to know more. His facial expression gave Ivy a chill. She held his hand and he jumped but compose himself quickly. Vins felt his wife's cold hand and rubbed it to make it warm. Ivy whispered to him to get her a blanket; she felt cold all of the sudden. While Vins went inside the house, Adelaide continue talking to Ivy about Tom, how she hated him because of what he did to her husband. She couldn't forget that coffee table incident.

Ivy wanted to tell Adelaide that Tom was her VIP client. She was not interested in his personal life. Ivy was aware of Tom's infatuation with her, but she was not interested. Seeing that Ivy wasn't responding to her, Adelaide stopped talking and turned her head towards the gazebo and the dock. She saw the kids giggling while holding a fishing rod, a fish dangling from the end. They were struggling to figure out how to manage it.

As the party went on, Ivy became aware of how clingy Vins was being. When he handed her the blanket, he caressed her and whispered sweet nothings into her ear. He said he liked how she smelled.

It was different for Ivy; she hated Vins's touch where she had loved it before. She felt tacky whenever he touched her, and claustrophobic when he sniffed her hair.

Adelaide saw them and she wished that Pierre could be as charming as Ivy's husband. Pierre never showed his affection when they were in public. Adelaide could tell that Ivy was annoyed with her husband but tolerating him anyway. Adelaide thought they were cute together.

At one point, Vins tried to squeeze next to Ivy on her chair, nearly knocking her over. She was afraid of what would happen to the baby if she fell; thankfully, she held onto the table.

Ethan came back to the terrace with Pierre, Tom, and Aunt Sue. Ivy's parents arrived soon after.

"Is that Suzanne McNae?" Daddy Todd said. Aunt Sue turned around and was surprised to see a familiar face. She had not expected to see Daddy Todd here, and she panicked a little.

"What the hell, how long has it been, thirty, forty years? You looked exactly the same as you did at the wedding and then I didn't see your family since," continued Daddy Todd. He also wasn't expecting to bump into her at this event. Daddy Todd was like a dormant volcano that had been quiet for a long time, then exploded. Everyone felt the anger and frustration emanating from his facial expression. Even Mommy Nas was shocked at his outburst.

The energy around the table had become intense, and everyone stared at Daddy Todd and Aunt Sue. They stopped eating and waited for an explanation.

"Vins, would you please show us to your study? We need to settle some issues in private. This might take a while, so please continue the celebration in our absence. Come with me, Suzanne. Nas, join us please. I want to know the truth now." Daddy Todd walked briskly towards the study; the two women followed him.

Ethan and Ivy had never experienced their dad's murderous stare. This was the first time they saw their dad loss his temper; his voice was so loud and strong that it gave them goosebumps. Vins had followed behind to guide them to the study, and Ethan gathered their plates and went after them.

"Pierre, do you know anything about this?" Tom asked. His cousin was older and might have more information about the relationship between Aunt Sue and Ivy's father.

Adelaide was also taken aback by the incident. She had no idea that her mother-in-law might have a past with Ivy's dad. She held Pierre's hand. Adelaide knew that his mom had been loyal to her deceased husband, even until today. Adelaide looked at Ivy; her face was blank. Ivy knew she needed to wait for her dad's explanation. She told everyone to continue eating and enjoy the party.

When Vins got back to the terrace and sat beside Ivy, he kissed her without warning; they bumped teeth and her lip started to bleed. Vins got scared when he saw the blood; he immediately got a tissue and wiped her lips. He couldn't stop apologizing and keep hugging Ivy. She wanted to punch her husband, but she didn't want to embarrass him in front of their guests.

To get him to stop pestering her, she grabbed his face and kissed him hard. She was annoyed but felt that she had to do it. Vins, on the other hand, was on cloud nine. He wanted all the guests to disappear so he could have sex with Ivy right there and then.

Pierre told Tom that he was surprised by what had happened. He suggested that they wait for the parents to come back. Pierre was confident that his mother had nothing to do with Ivy's father. Still, he glanced at Ethan, wondering if they could be related. He saw that Tom was staring at Ivy and Vins, clearly disgusted by their public displays of affection. He suggested that Tom go and help the children grill their fish.

Ivy was worried that she would get sick from the stench of the fish grilling, so she told Vins that she would like to take a rest in the master bedroom. She excused herself and Vins helped her into bed. He was so happy to finally be alone with his wife. But the moment she hit the bed, she fell asleep. Vins took off her shoes and tucked her in.

He was frustrated, but he continued to cuddle her. He laid down beside her and put his left arm under her head. He loved staring at her as she slept peacefully. It was like she was a magnet that kept pulling him in. After a while, his arm went numb, but he didn't want to move it and risk waking her.

He realized that he was being foolish. He had never been a clingy person, but the scent that his wife emitted was like a drug, and he was addicted. Her scent was his security. This had never happened to him, even when they were dating.

He knew that she had been put off by him when they were on the terrace. The feeling of rejection hit him hard, and he couldn't control his emotions. Right now, he had the chance to hold his wife, and he would make the best of it. She was staying over with her best friends, and he wanted them to have a wonderful time. Before Vins knew it, he had drifted off to sleep.

21

"TELL ME, IS THAT TOBIAS' son? Please do not lie to me, Suzanne. I want to know the truth!" Daddy Todd spoke in a low tone of voice but sounded irritated. He was sitting in an armchair in Vins's study. Aunt Sue and Mommy Nas were sitting beside each other on the couch.

Aunt Sue was a strong-willed person. She was an expert in controlling her emotions; still, she was afraid of the outcome of her conversation with Todd.

As for Nas, she was patient enough to wait for explanations. The woman beside her could be trusted; she did not look like she was capable of deception. She gave off the aura of an open book, as if she couldn't hide anything. Nas could feel that Sue was an honest person and would tell the truth when she was ready.

"I have no idea what is happening but I'm willing to listen to both of you, if that's why you asked me here," Nas said. "Always remember to talk without shouting; we need to stay calm even if it's hard to do. We won't get anywhere if we behave like lunatics." Todd and Sue both smiled at Nas. They knew this would take a while to figure out.

"Tobias is my half-brother," Daddy Todd began. "My mom had him after she came home from a trip to Africa. She had had a huge fight with my father over something petty, like young couples do. Unfortunately, my mother—ever the hopeless romantic— thought that if she ran away from my father, she could do whatever she liked. Bottom line, she met Tobias's dad, but it was a short-lived affair. She went back to Dad when she ran out of money, but she had no idea that she was pregnant.

Todd took a deep breath and went on. He explained that when his father found out that his wife was pregnant with someone else's child, he wanted to break her neck, throw her into the sea, and never see her again. But he loved her too much, so he accepted the child with open arms. His only request was that the child not to carry his last name. Todd's mom was devastated, but she also felt guilty; it was her fault, after all.

She agreed that Tobias would use her maiden name, Roye. Todd was five years older than Tobias; he loved his younger brother so much. He observed that their dad had no time for his brother, so Todd acted as a father to Tobias. When Todd went to University, Tobias was alone at home with their dad for the first time. Their mom was always out of the house at work. Tobias became a troubled child, but his stepfather never hurt him even if he was a trouble maker.

Todd's father was good in ignoring Tobias and acting as if he didn't exist. This drove Tobias to hate his mother for being so unfair to him. He loved his stepfather, even though he didn't acknowledge him. His stepfather was always there for Todd, even when he had nothing. Tobias wanted a father like that for his own, but he never knew who his real father was. When Todd went home for the holidays during his third year of university, he was surprised to find out that Tobias was getting married on Christmas day to Shannen McNae; they were both sixteen at that time. He felt that the marriage was unacceptable; his brother was too young to start his own family. Todd got a chance to talked to Tobias before the wedding. "The love I felt for Shannen was too deep to ignore and by marrying her will make me the luckiest person on earth!" Tobias told his brother with his face glowing with happiness. After hearing his brother explanation, Todd accepted Tobias decision to marry young.

The wedding was a small, intimate gathering. It was the first and last time Todd met Suzanne and the rest of Shannen's family. Todd never imagined that the wedding would also be the last time he would see his brother.

After the wedding, the McNae family brought Tobias to live at their home, thirty miles from the Dackers. Todd remembered that Christmas was the loneliest holiday he had ever experienced. He could see from his mom's facial expression that she felt relieved knowing that her son would live his own life and would not cause more trouble for her and her family.

On the other hand, his dad felt restless and keep asking if Tobias needed anything. He wanted to give Tobias money, but he could not face him. Todd couldn't explain how he felt; his mind was blank. Before Todd left to go back to school after the holidays, a friend of Tobias's dropped by their house and told him that Tobias was unhappy at home when Todd left for university. He missed his older brother. He could find strength from him, he said. Todd had been his rock all those years, even if he was only his half-brother. Their mom did not show him motherly love; it was only Todd who accepted him for what he was and loved him unconditionally. But he left him to study. So, when Tobias had a chance to leave the house through marriage, he swore that he would never set foot in their house again.

Daddy Todd stopped talking and looked up at Mommy Nas and Aunt Sue.

"Tobias asked me to promise him before he died that I would never introduce Tom to his family," Sue said. Her emotions were uncontrollable; she sobbed, and her tears blinded her. Nas gave her a tissue; she wiped her eyes and continued to tell her side of the story.

Shannen got pregnant with a honeymoon baby. Tobias was full of dreams for their upcoming child. Shannen and Suzanne's parents helped them to start up a clothing business right after the wedding. Shannen was an aspiring dressmaker and Tobias learned how to market his wife's creations. During those times, parties were the only way to have social gatherings. Young girls wanted to show off their new dresses on weekends, so between her studies and being pregnant, Shannen accepted orders. Her designs became famous within their circle.

After giving birth to Tom at seventeen, Shannen continued to make dresses, and she taught Tobias how to use their sewing machine. Tobias was an adaptive person, so he learned to sew and became a tailor. With their perseverance and love for each other, their business kept growing. They never imagined that their challenging work would give them a successful business. This business became their priority, and they left Tom with Sue every time the couple needed to travel to various places for their trade.

Tobias and Shannen became wealthy after only ten years in the business. On their eighteenth year, they were invited to give an inspirational talk at an entrepreneur summit up north. They were in a tragic car accident on the way, leaving Tom an orphan.

Sue got a call from the police up north, asking if she was related to Tobias Roye. She told him that she was his sister-in-law. Sue's world shattered and she panicked when she heard the police officer introduce himself over the phone. She could feel her heart drop from her chest, and her imagination ran wild.

When she tried to calm herself to ask the person on the other line what had happen, she heard a hoarse, soft voice saying, "Take care of Tom and never to show him to my family." Sue pressed the receiver towards her ear because she couldn't make out what the other person was saying, then she realized it was Tobias who was talking. Sue asked him what had happened and where he was, but there was no response.

Then she heard the police officer saying, "Sorry for your loss, he did not make it." Sue shouted at the police officer and asked him where to find her sister, but the police officer told her that Shannen hadn't made it too.

Suzanne woke up with her family around her. Her husband said that she passed out and had been sleeping for ten hours. Paule grabbed his mom's hands and held them tight. Her husband whispered to her that Tom had no idea what had happened.

Two days later when their bodies had been sent home, Aunt Sue told Tom what had happened to his parents.

"So, tell me, what would you do if you were the one who got that call?" Sue said. "I had to respect Tobias's last wish."

Todd couldn't hold back his tears and had turned his back on Sue and Nas to hide his emotions.

"After all these years, my feelings of abandonment are still fresh in my heart," Todd said. "If it was not for Nas and my kids, I would never have been happy again without Tobias. I went to university so that I could support him, but I never told him that. So, he found a different way to escape. I want to acknowledge Tom as my nephew, Suzanne. Please let me introduce myself to him. I don't know what the outcome of this revelation will be, but I want to try to know him and for Tom to know me and my family.

"I know he's infatuated with my daughter," Todd went on. "I saw how he admired Ivy. We need to let him know that she is his first cousin, not a love interest. His blood is the same as my daughter's blood. Hopefully, he will understand why he has been feeling this way towards Ivy. Are you willing to let me do that, Suzanne?"

Suzanne felt the emptiness of Todd's heart; she could deny Tobias's dying wish to heal the broken hearts of his family. She nodded.

"Nas, please call the kids, but spare Ivy from this matter," Todd said. "I don't want her to stress herself during this time." Nas stood up gave Daddy Todd a kiss. She hugged Suzanne and thanked her, then she went downstairs to do as Todd had asked.

When she approached the table where Ethan, Tom, Pierre, and Adelaide were sitting, she asked Tom and Ethan to join them in the study, leaving Pierre and Adelaide confused. They didn't ask what was going on, but they were concerned.

"Where is your sister, Ethan?" Nas asked. She peered into the half-opened glass door of the master bedroom. She saw the couple sleeping while embracing. It was nice to see them close to each other. She has no idea how her daughter could tolerate the roller coaster ride of a relationship with her mentally unstable husband. Tom looked in and saw same scene that Mommy Nas saw. He felt angry seeing Ivy with Vins. It should be him.

Ethan was confused about why he had been summoned to the study with Tom, and he didn't like it. Though his mother seemed calm, which made him feel a little better. Watching the kids play earlier, his head had been filled with thoughts of happy years spent with family. Then he thought about what would happen to his sister when Vins found out she was pregnant.

Ethan was leaving for Malaysia in two days' time, and Ivy needed someone to stay with her twenty-four/seven now that she's pregnant. Ethan glanced into the master bedroom and hoped that Vins and his sister would make a wise decision about their marriage. They need to consider the baby in his sister's belly.

When Ethan, Nas, and Tom arrived in the study, Aunt Sue started talking immediately.

"Tom, when you were growing up, you only knew your relatives from your mother's side of the family," she said. "Your dad never mentioned anyone from his side. I know in your heart you've always wanted to ask me about it, but you stayed quiet. I never lied to you about anything, and you know that, right? You grew up a happy child but along the way, you experienced the loss of your parents and became troubled. But you bounced back and became a successful businessman. I hope you can open your life to your father's side of the family. There's always a reason things happen or why we met people at the right time, and sometimes at the wrong place."

Surprised by what Aunt Sue was saying, Tom glanced around the room at the people in the study and wondered what was going on. He was shocked by what he heard, but at the same time he was excited to know that he still had living relatives from his father's side. Tom ran his fingers through his hair. Suddenly, he lost control of his emotions.

"What is happening, Auntie? Please explain because I'm tipsy from the beer and wine and I can't absorb anything. I feel lonely seeing Ivy sleeping with her husband and embracing him."

His feelings of rejection hurt him so much. He looked fragile and unwanted. He may have been tall, but he felt small.

"Sorry Ethan, Mr. & Mrs. Dacker, I think I'm too drunk and that's why I said those things. I confess that I like Ivy and hopefully she will be my wife."

Tom felt ashamed as he realized how he had been treating Ivy. His world seemed to revolve around her in that moment. He was at loss, scared to know the truth about his father's family. Aunt Sue's calm voice echoed in his ears; he felt dizzy and restless, and he wanted to sit down.

She chuckled after she heard what Tom said, "That's why you need to know your true relationship with Ivy and Ethan, Tom," Aunt Sue said. "Be still, Tom,"

Daddy Todd was impatient to speak, so he interrupted Aunt Sue and explained the details of the situation to Tom.

"Tom, your dad, Tobias, was my half-brother," Todd said. "We shared the same mother. When I saw Suzanne with you earlier when you arrived, I immediately know who you were. Your dad was my only sibling and knowing that he was your father, I felt relieved that at last, you are home. My brother and me had the best relationship when we were younger until I left for university, and he thought I would no longer be a part of his life. I thought after the wedding we would go back to normal, but he left with your mother and never came back to see his family. I felt empty after that; my life was never the same until I had my own family."

Ethan was shocked. He didn't know how to react. He had never held a grudge toward Tom, but the fact that Tom was infatuated with Ivy made Ethan sick to his stomach. He hoped that Tom would understand now that his love for Ivy was inappropriate.

As for Mommy Nas, she was glad that her husband had finally found his nephew, even after so many years. Fate was testing them to accept the present after they had been surprised by the past.

Ethan was aware that his mother had never liked Tom since the first time she saw him ogling her daughter in Singapore, but she was willing to forget the past and create new memories in the present for Todd's sake. Aunt Sue sat beside Tom on the loveseat and held his hands in hers.

"I know this was hard to hear, especially because of your feelings for Ivy," she said. "But you're a grown man, and you still have plenty of time to find love. Your feelings for Ivy are feelings of love for a relative. This is your truth, and you must accept it. You've gained not only her, but your entire family, Tom."

Tom started to sob and hugged his auntie. So, this was his truth, and he was not dreaming. This is for real.

22

IVY WAS STARTLED WHEN SHE woke up to the sound of loud voices and shouting from upstairs. She was not fully awake when she realized that she had fallen asleep, and someone was embracing her tightly. She hated the scent of the person hugging her, but it was a familiar scent that she used to love.

Gradually opening her eyes, she was surprised to see Vins sleeping next to her with a serene expression on his face. Even with his eyes closed, she could see that he was at peace. They seldom took naps together; she liked the idea but felt suffocated and irritated. She wanted to get up because her bladder was full, but Vins's arm was around her waist, and she had a tough time lifting it. Her bladder was making her uncomfortable, so she decided to push on his arm. Her annoyance was visible on her face.

"Vins wake up, I need to go to the washroom. Hey, please wake up." Ivy's voice was vibrating through Vins's eardrums. Surprised by the sudden push on his arm and his wife's loud voice, Vins sat up and immediately checked to see that Ivy was okay.

She saw his face became pale and confused. She wanted to laugh because she had never seen her husband that scared in their entire married life. Ivy started to get up, but she felt her stomach was not cooperating and wanted to puke. She didn't want Vins to figure out she was pregnant, so she moved cautiously towards the bathroom.

Vins got up and checked the backyard; everyone was taking their nap or having a drink near the dock. No kids' laughter or bantering. The lake house was calm and quiet. He had heard shouting earlier coming from upstairs, but he thought he must have been dreaming. Then he heard the sound of sobbing coming from his study. He wanted to go see what was going on right away, but when Ivy emerged from the bathroom, she was so pale that it frightened him. He rushed to her and held her, helping her make her way to the recliner. He handed her a bottle of water.

"Are you all right? You look terrible. Do you want me to call your mom?" Vins asked.

"What are you saying? I feel fine, it was just the food that I ate earlier, maybe it was spoiled or something. I feel relieved after getting it out from my system. Go check on our guests and please ask the caterers to serve dinner on the long table. It will be night soon and I love to see the stars while having dinner. We can ask the guests to stay for the night if they want it. Billy and Sam's family can stay with us in the master bedroom so that the other guests can use the three bedrooms upstairs. Ethan's crew would love to set up the tents near the lake. In two days, they will be heading to Malaysia, and they'll miss autumn nights like this one. I'm happy to see my brother is enjoying this moment with them, not working and just having the best time of their lives." Ivy avoided Vins's gaze as she spoke.

When Vins had left, Ivy called Billy and asked him to go and find her mom. Billy was watching his twins sleep while reading a book; he had heard the commotion coming from the study, but had ignored it, knowing it was none of his business.

After he hung up, he went to the study and knocked on the door. He could still hear sobbing coming from inside, so he called to Mommy Nas, saying that Ivy was looking for her. Mommy Nas knew that Ivy was being careful not to go upstairs so as not to strain herself. But it was time she knew what had happened, so Mommy Nas made her way downstairs. Sam and Brianna were taking a nap when Sam heard the sobbing from the other bedroom. Before going down, she made sure that Brianna was still sleeping. Sam went into the master bedroom and saw Ivy caressing her tummy. She was glowing, and her smile was breathtaking.

"The magic glow of a pregnant woman really is beautiful," she said, giving Ivy a hug.

"Billy and I will make sure that both of you will be safe and have a happy home, babe. Nobody can take that away from you. Your baby will give you another chance to create a new and lasting relationship. Life has new meaning for you." Sam smiled and kissed Ivy on the cheek. Ivy didn't notice that her eyes were wet while listening to her best friend. She believed what Sam said, she's lucky to have her friends. Her baby would be the apple of their eyes and would grow up with a loving family. She would make sure that would be their reality. Her hormones were working overtime, and she continued crying while talking to Sam about their future.

Sam was crying, too, though it was because of her own misery and not Ivy's joy. The two women held each other, their shoulders shaking with sobs. They didn't realize that Mommy Nas had come into the room. Mommy Nas seldom cried in front of her family, but seeing Sam and Ivy, and after everything that had just happened, she started sobbing, too. She went to the bathroom and brought out wet towels to help with the redness in their eyes. The girls laughed when they realized Mommy Nas was there and told her they were crying happy tears.

Mommy Nas filled them in about the state of the party; the caterers had set everything up and would start serving food in one hour. Daddy Todd was going to make a big announcement during dinner. She didn't tell them what it would be; that was Todd's task for the night.

The lake house backyard was beautiful at night. The opposite side of the lake was dark. The only light was coming from the small boats that were passing by. The gazebo where the food was being served was lit up with string lights and warmed by heaters. The dock area was also well-lit.

Vins had chosen different coloured lights to form a perimeter around the dining area. They would unplug the lights later when it was time for stargazing. The ducks were loud as they made their way back to their nests for the night. The kids loved to watch the ducks pass by and feed bread crumbs to them.

Ethan's crew had set up their tents near the portable heaters; they had also changed their clothes and were ready for dinner. Vins had been doubtful that he would enjoy the company of Ethan's crew; he wasn't a people person. But the crew was down-to-earth, and Vins found himself liking them. He felt proud of his brother-in-law, which confused him even more. He had never liked Ethan from the start. Vins was possessive and didn't want to share his wife with her family.

The long table was big enough for twenty-four people, the autumn-themed plates, glass, and cutlery were in place. The caterer had used burlap placemats. Autumn leaves were scattered around the long table, and votive candles were flickering under the cold autumn night sky. Orange and green blankets had been placed on each chair. The scent of smoking logs from the fire pits lingered on the wind. The atmosphere were festive.

The kids' table was placed near the gazebo not far from the adult table. The caterer announced that dinner would be served in ten minutes. Mommy Nas went upstairs and informed her family and Sue that dinner would soon be served. Tom was still not back to his old self but managed to nod. Aunt Sue was embarrassed by his actions; he never drank that much.

Daddy Todd squeezed Tom's shoulder and patted Ethan's back. He and Ethan went downstairs, leaving Tom with Aunt Sue. Tom went into the washroom to freshen up. He tried to remember what had just happened, but he couldn't comprehend that Ivy was his family. He was afraid to face her, knowing how rude and blunt he had been towards her.

"Divorce him for me," he remembered saying to her at the airport. Stupid move on his part. He hated himself for that. He was thankful to Ethan, who had accepted him, though Tom wouldn't have thought that was possible after how he had behaved. Even Mommy Nas had acknowledged him as family. Life was testing him. He had been successful in business but not in his personal life. In his mind, Ivy was the definition of the perfect wife and mother. Could he ever find another woman like her?

Tom was struggling to decide if he was willing to accept this reality. He wasn't worried about his business relationship with Ivy, at least; they understood that business was business. They still needed to discuss the down jackets that Ivy was in the process of producing.

"Dad, could you not announce our relationship with Tom tonight? I have my crew members here and I don't want them to know about my personal life. I'm just being careful about our family affairs," Ethan asked his dad while they were walking downstairs. He suggested to his father to invite Aunt Sue and Tom to join them at Ivy's house tomorrow. It was more private and only family would be there. He would invite Pierre and Paule as well. Daddy Todd understood his son's concerns and agreed to hold off on the announcement.

Tonight, was about Ethan's championship win. Daddy Todd couldn't hide his happiness. When he saw Sam at the table, he hugged her. Sam was taken aback and wanted to push Daddy Todd away before she realized who he was. She turned around and gave him a peck on the cheek. Her laughter was so contagious that Ivy laughed, too. Even Billy didn't escape Daddy Todd's playfulness. He got a kiss from Daddy Todd, which he reciprocated. The atmosphere at the long table was wonderful.

Vins loved Ivy's laugh. She gave off a beautiful aura that radiated from her soul. Before the caterer served their dinner, Daddy Todd, who was sitting at the head of the table, raised his wine glass and gave a toast to congratulate his son for winning the championship. He spoke about Ethan's love of cars and his passion for car racing. He even mentioned how Ivy was inspired by his brother's passion for cars. Daddy Todd also included in his speech how his wife supported their children's dreams; he was thankful to her for being an awesome mother. Daddy Todd got emotional and had tears in his eyes, but he explained that they were happy tears.

Dinner was served. Ivy sat at the centre of the table. She had Vins to her right and Sam to her left, with Billy sitting next to Vins. The dinner was marvelous, and everyone loved how the food was cooked. The kids were served pasta and chicken strips with chocolate cake and hot chocolate. They couldn't get enough of their s'mores. When they were done eating, Billy wrapped them in blankets and brought them to the tent for stargazing.

The adults were also done with dinner and were drinking their wine. Ivy whispered something to Sam's and they both got up and made their way to the master bedroom from the terrace.

"My stomach isn't cooperating with me; I feel like puking again. This is so hard; I'm scared, Sam. I don't know what to do." Ivy started to cry. Sam couldn't hold back her tears, either. She was under so much stress that her emotions felt unbearable. She went into the bathroom to calm herself, then called Mommy Nas.

Mommy Nas felt her daughter's pain. She rubbed her back and assured her that it would pass. She asked Ivy if she was still planning to hide the pregnancy from Vins. Ivy had no idea if she could, but she knew she needed to protect her baby from her husband. Ivy embraced her mother as if she was just a little girl again.

This pregnancy had given her a new perspective on her relationship with her mom. Mommy Nas embraced her daughter and kissed her forehead. She wanted Ivy to know that she would support her all the way. Ivy knew that her parents would be excellent grandparents; she had had the best childhood that anyone could ask for. Ivy panicked just thinking about what would happen if Vins found out she was pregnant. She had learned her lesson during her first two miscarriages that he would likely try to intentionally terminate the pregnancy by force.

"Let's go back to the table, everyone is looking for you," Mommy Nas said. "I could see from their faces that they were grateful that you hosted Ethan's party here. They enjoyed the lake and all the things they've done today. As for your husband, I could see how clingy he was to you. I'm thinking maybe he has some pregnancy symptoms, too. He seemed to be feeling helpless and wanted to touch you every time you were near him." Mommy Nas chuckled.

Mommy Nas talked about how Daddy Todd had acted the same way when she was pregnant with Ivy. She didn't have morning sickness, but he vomited every day for three months. He didn't think he could handle another pregnancy. Mommy Nas thought that maybe

Vins was experiencing something like that. Ivy laughed at her mom's story, and thought her dad was cute and lovable. Her heart bled for Vins, but he had a demon inside him. She needed to be on guard at all times to keep her baby safe.

Sam felt her heart shatter as she listened to Mommy Nas and Ivy. She remembered how Robby had denied her a second pregnancy. Sam wanted to share her experience with the two women, but she was afraid to tell the truth. She pulled herself together and held Ivy's hand, saying they should go back to the party and the stargazing.

They went outside and were met by Shelley, who couldn't control her excitement. "Mom Ivy, you and Uncle Vins have the best house in the world! Please invite us again. I don't think Lucas will ever stop talking about stargazing after tonight. He was so quiet watching the stars; he said monsters were looking at us! But I'm a big girl and I don't believe in monsters. Daddy, please tell Mom Ivy to invite us again, please, please, Daddy?"

Vins's heart softened towards the girl. He invited her to come sit with him and Ivy and tell them when she wanted to visit. Ivy could hardly believe her eyes; Vins hated children and couldn't stand to be around them. Was it possible that he actually had parental instincts after all?

"This by far was the most relaxed and best celebration that we have attended in the past ten years," Pierre said. "Cheers to that. And Dacker, you, my man, are the fiercest but safest driver I've ever known in my entire life. I had no idea that you also had the most lovable family. Thank you for sharing this side of your life with us. My hat's off to you and I hope we will work together as long as you're driving."

Ivy had no idea if Pierre was drunk or just happy to see her brother's soft side. She didn't regret celebrating his win at the lake house. Ivy picked up her glass of water and made a toast to Pierre. All this time, Tom was sitting opposite Ivy and staring at her. He could not react and did nothing. Ivy had no idea that they were cousins.

She was still waiting for her dad's announcement, but nothing happened. After the toast, Ethan stood and shook hands with Pierre and the crew.

Everyone was staying the night. As the caterer cleaned up, everyone made their way to their rooms. Billy had purchased air mattresses so there would be plenty of room.

It was eleven p.m. when Ivy realized that her mother-in-law hadn't joined their celebration. She had forgotten about her in all the commotion. She asked Vins what had happened.

"I forgot to tell you," he said. "She called me earlier. Her car broke down and she sent it to the repair shop. I will pick her up tomorrow and drive her to your place for Ethan's farewell dinner."

Ivy checked on the kids, who by that time were sleeping peacefully in their sleeping bags. They were like angels; Brianna was laughing while she dreamed.

Sam and Billy were sitting on the terrace. Looking at them, Ivy sensed that something was wrong. Billy was holding Sam's shoulder and she was leaning on his chest.

They were the most lovable people Ivy knew. She hoped that Sam would open up to her, too, but she doubted it; she knew Sam would be careful not to cause her extra stress now that Ivy was pregnant.

Ivy looked at Vins, who was sitting by her side. *He's the love of my life and I'm afraid of him,* she thought.

23

IVY WOKE UP THE NEXT morning feeling exhausted, with an unexplainable ache in her heart. Her husband was sleeping beside her. Ivy was confused and couldn't keep still; she wanted to get out of bed. Suddenly, Vins reached out in his sleep and touched her belly. She was startled and couldn't control her tears. Her world was collapsing because of the mixed signals Vins was sending her.

Vins had been so attentive to her needs since Ethan had arrived, even when they weren't together. Maybe he sensed that he would soon be a father, though Ivy had no idea how he really felt about her. She warned herself that this was not the right time for Vins to be in her life. He would ruin everything the moment he found out about the baby.

Ivy felt like shoving his arm off her, but she didn't want to wake him. She stayed still and allowed his arm to rest on her belly. Right now, it was flat, but she knew a bump would soon be showing. She caressed Vins's arm; he moved a little but didn't wake up.

Ethan drove her car going home. Ivy was restless and annoyed in the passenger seat; she never imagined that her brother would be driving her Mini. Her frustration was killing her, so she shut her eyes and tried to nap. She was bloated, and they had to stop at a gas station three times along the way because of her morning sickness.

Ivy missed her mother-in-law. She was so thoughtful and generous with her time. Mama Belle would be a wonderful grandmother.

When they arrived at home, Ethan carried Ivy to her bedroom. Mommy Nas had prepared the room so that Ivy could rest before dinner. She felt accomplished when she saw how her children took care of each other. With her husband's love and dedication and her pride in her children, she was happy with her family life.

Thoughts of her younger years were still clear in Mommy Nas's mind. She had strict parents and seldom laughed; that's how her children knew her. After their trip to Singapore, she saw that the life she was living now was so wonderful, and she opened herself up to them and allowed them to know that there was another side of her.

In Mommy Nas's household, her father always had the final say. Nobody complained, even if her mother felt oppressed and disrespected. Her father worked hard to send his children to school. His main goal was for his children to be educated. He told them that education was important for their well-being. Mommy Nas never attended social gatherings; her daily routine was to go to school, then go home do some household chores, finish her homework, early to bed. When she graduated from college, she worked as the town librarian until she married Todd.

Todd was a dashing son of a land owner. They were well-off and he had been sent to study at the big university. He was the town's ultimate bachelor, and when he fell in love with the strict and reserved librarian, his parents did not expect that the relationship would last. But they saw that Todd was head-over-heels in love with Nas, so they approved of the marriage.

Now, Nas showed her family that she had changed her attitude towards her future grandkids. She was so excited to finally meet the baby in six months' time. Mommy Nas planned to pay extra attention to Ivy to help her have a successful pregnancy. She told her husband that they would go home the next day after's Ethan's departure and get what they needed to come back and stay with Ivy for the duration of her pregnancy.

Ivy was cautious walking down the stairs; she was all dressed up for dinner. She was wearing a wrap-around top in white—her favourite colour—with loose, brown pique pants. The V-neck collar of her top exposed her chest a little bit and she brought a cardigan just in case she felt cold. On her neck was the diamond necklace Ethan gave her for her wedding. The autumn weather was getting colder every day.

Mommy Nas saw Ivy coming down the stairs and rushed toward her. She was scared that Ivy might slip because she was wearing socks. Ivy showed her mom that her socks had anti-slip to prevent slipping. Mama Belle saw how Mommy Nas was concerned about Ivy, and she wondered why.

Ivy saw Mama Belle and smiled. She gave her a hug and told her how much she had missed her. Mama Belle was grateful; Ivy really was a good girl, and she hoped that her son would open his eyes and see that for himself soon. If not, he would lose a wonderful person. Mama Belle thought that Ivy's eyes were sad, but her smile was genuine. She asked Ivy what she had brought back from Singapore. Mommy Nas mentioned that the expensive satchel bag she had bought was a gift from Mama Belle. Ivy's face lit up when she remembered the bag that she hadn't been able to afford. She thought Mommy Nas had been too generous when she paid for the bag; all this time, it was from Mama Belle.

Vins came inside from the garage carrying a case of beer. When he saw his wife, he couldn't hide his happiness. He was beaming with pride, his eyes almost shut from smiling. He put the beer in the fridge then walked over to Ivy, squeezing her cheeks, and hugging her so tightly that she could hardly breathe.

"Stop killing your wife with your embrace!" Mama Belle said, and the other parents laughed.

Ivy gently pushed her husband away and tried to catch her breath. Mommy Nas saw the discomfort on Ivy's face and helped her sit down on the armchair in the living room.

Mama Belle and Mommy Nas were busy preparing a dinner of all the comfort foods their kids had loved since childhood. They hoped Tom's family would enjoy it, too. Mama Belle had been briefed about Tom when she arrived. She felt emotional hearing the story of Todd's family.

Her imagination was worked up. Sometimes, fate was ruthless, but knowing the truth was more painful.

The mothers were happy to be having this family gathering. Mama Belle was joyful to see her son having a great time with his wife and in-laws. The Dackers seemed to have forgotten what Vins did to Ivy. The atmosphere was really homey. Ethan even set up the home theatre in case they wanted to watch a movie. Their guests arrived on time. Tom, Aunt Sue, Paule, and Pierre were all there, though Adelaide wasn't able to join them.

Paule and Pierre greeted Ivy and sat down on the couch in front of the fireplace. Ivy felt a sting in her heart when Paule gave her a smile. She dismissed the feeling and tried to locate Vins. Ethan came back from the kitchen and offered them drinks and some nuts to nibble on. Mommy Nas and Daddy Todd welcomed them.

Vins, on the other hand, was helping his mom toss the garden salad. He kept checking on Ivy and felt a sudden tingling sensation on his skin when he saw Ivy yawn while staring at him. His wife was stunning, even if she was not in the mood to smile lately. Vins was puzzled by her mood swings; he never knew her to be grumpy.

The dining table was filled with food: green salad, bacon, and cheese perogies, roasted dill salmon, roast beef, mashed potatoes, pork chops, and roasted vegetables. Mommy Nas made chili and bacon soup to satisfy Ivy's cravings. She avoided cooking with too much garlic or oil.

Dinner was served at exactly six p.m. Ivy sat in the middle with Vins and Ethan on either side of her. Mommy Nas and Mama Belle sat to her left. Opposite of Ivy was Daddy Todd, and on his left were Tom and Paule, with Aunt Sue and Pierre on his right.

Tom sat opposite Vins, and everyone could feel the tension between the two people who loved Ivy.

After the prayers, Daddy Todd thanked Ivy and Vins for hosting the gathering.

"Ivy," he said, "I think you're the only person here tonight who has no idea why we are gathered here today. Let me introduce to you your cousin, son of my long-lost half-brother Tobias. Tom Roye is my nephew, though I had no idea that he existed until yesterday when I saw him with Aunt Sue. I think you'll be relieved to know that this annoying gentleman is actually your cousin." He chuckled.

Nobody could control their laughter. Tom was praying that the floor would swallow him alive he was so embarrassed. His face turned crimson, and he awkwardly joined in the laughter.

He gathered his courage and stood up. "I'm sorry Ivy. I had a hard time understanding my love for you. In the end, it was love for a relative. Don't get me wrong, I still admire you." Tom winked at Ivy and raised his wine glass for a toast.

Ivy did not expect this turn of events, and she had no idea how to react. She stared at her dad; she needed to know everything in order to believe that this was really happening. She had no idea that her VIP client was her cousin.

Daddy Todd knew what Ivy was thinking. "We'll give you all the details soon enough. For now, let's just enjoy our time together as a family," he said, and he offered a welcoming toast to Tom.

"Welcome to the family, and feel free to join us for future celebrations," Vins said. "Thank you for loving my beautiful wife, even if she never noticed you." He smirked. Tom stopped eating out of embarrassment.

Ivy told Vins to stop teasing Tom, but soon all the cousins were teasing him, and everyone had dissolved into laughter. Mama Belle got up and hugged him, asking him to forgive her son. "You poor kid!"

Tom stood up again and made a toast. "I expect that you all will never stop teasing me about this, right? Well, let me offer an apology to you, Ivy. I'm sorry for hitting on you and asking you to do something that I know you would never do. A toast to all of our personal happiness and contentment. Thank you all for the warm welcome; now I have my cousins from my mother's and father's sides with me.

"Aunt Sue, thank you for always believing in me. Uncle Todd and Auntie Nas, thank you for showing me that blood is indeed thicker than water. I'm overwhelmed with emotions, so thank you for tonight." He savoured his wine.

As they settled back to their meal, Daddy Todd asked Aunt Sue, "Suzanne, did Tobias kept the blue sedan that my father gave me for my high school graduation? I gave it to him as a wedding gift because I knew he needed it more than I did."

Aunt Sue was caught off-guard by the question. She seemed unable to speak and glanced at Tom, who had turned white as a sheet, as if the blood had been drained from his body. "What is it, Tom?" Mommy Nas asked. "You look like you just saw a ghost." She handed him a glass of water, and she felt scared.

Tom was panicked; the house seemed to grow dark with emotions flooding the room. Everybody stopped what they were doing, as if time stood still. The room was silent except for the sound of breathing.

"The blue sedan you're talking about had a dent on the left bumper, right?" Vins said. He was staring at his father-in-law, his face dark with anger and his right hand curled into a fist. "It had a bumper sticker that said, 'Heaven on Earth,' and the license plate number was 12A B54."

Vins had the same expression on his face as when he had assaulted Ivy three months prior. She was too scared to look at him, but she had to do something to keep him from becoming violent in front of her family. She grabbed him by the wrist and told him to calm down, but he shoved her hand away. Mama Belle got between them, as if to protect Ivy from her son.

When Daddy Todd didn't answer, Vins continued. "Tom were you the one driving that car on the night of September fifth, twenty years ago?" Aunt Sue started wailing and became hysterical to the point of melting down. Her biggest fear—the truth being discovered—was happening right in front of her. She remembered what her husband had said twenty years ago: "The truth will always come out, no matter how carefully a person hides it." Pierre and Paule were shaken seeing their mom in that state. She was their rock and shield, a superwoman, but the simplest question about the blue sedan made her weak. Neither of them had any idea what Vins was talking about.

"Answer me now," Vins yelled. His voice was aggressive and intense. Then, without warning, he jumped over the table and grabbed Tom by the throat, choking him. Food was splattered across the table and Tom fell to the floor.

Vins's hands were around Tom's neck and Tom was turning blue. Vins was so angry; there was no doubt that he would kill Tom if nobody intervened. It was Paule who jumped up and tried to pull the men apart.

"Get off your hands off him, you'll kill him!" he shouted, grabbing Vins by the shoulder. But Vins was too strong and kicked Paule away. Ethan and Pierre snapped out of their state of shock and tried to subdue Vins. The room dissolved into pandemonium.

Afraid for Ivy's safety, Daddy Todd shouted at Mommy Nas to take her away from the chaos. Vins's adrenaline was so strong that the three men had a hard time controlling him. His veins were popping out and his grip was nearly unbreakable. Tom's eyes were starting to close, and they were afraid that he would not make it out of this ordeal alive. "Please, Belle, do something!" Aunt Sue pleaded with Mama Belle. "Don't let your son make the same mistake my nephew did twenty years ago!"

"I had no idea about the blue sedan, Sue. Was that the same car that killed my husband?" Mama Belle was trembling, her face red with anger. She looked like Vins when she was mad. Her hoarse voice vibrated through the house.

Hearing his mother, Vins snapped out of his anger. He let go of Tom and pushed him away, then ran to his mother. She was sitting on the floor and sobbing, cradling her knees. Vins was worried about his mother; she never mourned her husband's death because she wanted to stay strong for her son. Her emotions were overflowing.

Ivy was on her way up the stairs with her mother when she heard Mama Belle scream. She couldn't bear to leave her mother-in-law when she was so upset. Forgetting about her pregnancy, she ran back down the stairs and fell to the floor with Mama Belle, comforting her. Vins picked up his phone and called the police. "Bring Sheriff Berns here now," he said. "We'll explain everything when you arrive."

24

"IVY, DON'T MOVE," VINS SAID. "I want everyone to listen to me. Tonight, will be my night. I've been living in hell for the past twenty years because of my father's untimely death. It was one of your family who killed him. Mama, we will have justice for Papa. You and I will finally be able to move on from our grief." Vins's eyes were red and scary. His gaze gave Ivy goosebumps. She was confused and continued to hold Mama Belle.

Mommy Nas tried to help Mama Belle onto the couch to make her comfortable, but Mama Belle refused. Ethan helped Tom into a chair while Pierre and Paule discussed what their next move would be if Vins's accusations about Tom were true. Looking at their mother, they knew that it was the truth. Aunt Sue had stopped crying but her body was still trembling. Daddy Todd had no idea what to do except wait and listen.

Meanwhile, at Sam's house, her husband Robby had gotten a phone call.

"Where are you going?" she asked. "Why did Vins called you? I had no idea that you even had his number. We're in the middle of dinner and you're just leaving?" Sam was shocked to know that her husband was that close with Vins. They had never interacted much before, even when they bumped into each other. She had no idea why Vins had called him at this hour.

Robby's facial expression was fierce while he was talking to Vins. He wasn't finished eating, but the moment he hung up the phone, he immediately left the dining table and went to their bedroom to change. When he emerged, he was furious with Sam. He grabbed her by the throat and choked her.

"You have no right to ask me to do anything. You are just my wife. I could kill you anytime, so stop pestering me. You need to shut up and ignore everything I do if you want to live in peace." Robby was raging and talking wildly. Then he went to the garage to get his car and dialled Sheriff Berns's mobile number, telling him to bring his deputy with him to Vins and Ivy's residence as soon as possible. "This is the day we've been waiting for, for the last ten years!" Robby shouted as he drove to Ivy's house.

Sam called Billy and told him everything that had happened. "He's on his way to Ivy's house now," she said. "We need to go there. I'll drop Brianna off with her nanny and you do the same. I'll never forgive Robby for how he treated me tonight."

Brianna was afraid after seeing what her father had done. She could sense that she was in danger, but she knew her Mommy Sam would protect her no matter what. She got ready and met her mother at the front door, hugging her and kissing her face.

After dropping the kids off, Billy and Sam supported each other by hugging and rubbing each other's backs to show that they were in this together. They had no idea on what to expect at Ivy's house. They knew that her family was hosting Tom's family that night. They couldn't understand why Robby would rush out after Vins's call; the two men had only met thrice.

Robby arrived at Ivy's house. He waited for the sheriff and his deputy to arrive before ringing the doorbell. Ethan greeted them and let them in. His face was haggard, and his clothes were wrinkly after all the commotion.

The sheriff and his deputy walked in along with Robby. Mama Belle was still on the floor with Ivy. Broken dishes were scattered all around and tension was thick in the air. Mama Belle was still sobbing.

Daddy Todd stood up from the dining chair and extended his hand to the sheriff. The deputy's professional eyes were scanning the scene, though he didn't touch anything. They had no arrest warrant or search warrant. Their visit was just a house call. But they had to be vigilant and must keep their visit professional.

"Sheriff, Deputy, we had a family dinner," Daddy Todd said. "We were welcoming my nephew into the family; I didn't know he existed until recently because of family issues in the past. My son-in-law, Vins, discovered that my nephew was the one who committed the hit and run that killed his father twenty years ago. Vins couldn't control his emotions and choked my nephew, resulting in the broken dishes you see on the floor. Tom never admitted his guilt out loud, but based on his reaction, it might be true. That's why Vins asked Robby to call you here."

Daddy Todd was scared for his nephew and of what might happen to him. Vins asked the sheriff to sit on the couch in the living room. He told him what he had seen during the hit and run when he was a teen. The sheriff listened while his deputy took down the statement. Ivy and Mama Belle sat in the armchairs near the fireplace. The Dackers stayed in the dining room, except for Daddy Todd, who was also in the living room.

Pierre and Paule were comforting Tom, who was troubled and had no idea what would happen to him. Mommy Nas stayed by Aunt Sue's side.

The doorbell rang; Paule had called a defense attorney, who had just arrived. Paule greeted him and told him to follow him to the dining room, then briefed him about the incident.

After hearing about the case, the lawyer assured Paule that he would assist them with whatever they needed to keep Tom out of prison. He said that the incident happened a long time ago when Tom was just a teenager, so he may not be tried as an adult. The lawyer then talked to Tom in private. He was still in pain after being choked. Aunt Sue told him to be honest this time and to face the consequences of his actions. It would be better to correct his mistake now. She assured Tom that they would do their best to keep him safe and keep his business going.

As for Pierre, he was afraid that Tom would go off the deep end. He saw how his cousin had struggled when they were younger. He wished that things could have turned out the way they wanted. No running anymore.

While Pierre and Paule were talking, Billy and Sam rushed in and were surprised at what they saw. They felt the tension in the room instantly. Ivy's face was so pale, as if she was really worried. Sam looked at Robby and wanted to talk to him, but Robby ignored her while standing behind Vins as if he was guarding him with his life. Who was Vins to her Robby?

"We need to bring Mr. Roye to the police station now, and if you want to lay charges you can come along with us, Mr. Reynolds," Sheriff Berns said. Tom's lawyer agreed, reassuring Tom's family that he would look into the case thoroughly.

"Bring him in, Sheriff Berns," Vins said. "I need to talk to my wife and her family then I will follow you to the station. I need to clear something up with them before I leave. Robby stay with me."

Ivy's parents were confused; they had no idea what was happening. As for Sam, she had no idea that her husband was Detective Robby Smithe. He never told her his job; she knew that he worked, because he left their house daily before eight a.m, and came home before six p.m. Sometimes, he would leave home after office hours and come home two days later. Sam asked where he was going, but Robby would simply reply, "Duty calls," then turn his back and walk away. Sam never doubted his honesty and sincerity until their relationship devolved.

She was at a loss. Her world had shattered into pieces once again. Life was a roller coaster ride for her and her family. Love was uncertain.

Aunt Sue's family left with the sheriff and his deputy, leaving Ivy with her family and her two best friends. Aunt Sue couldn't stop crying; Pierre helped her to the car. Paule drove himself to the station.

Tom didn't struggle when the police brought him out of the house. He sighed while sitting at the back of the police car. This was his worst nightmare, and he wanted to go to sleep and never wake up. His life was starting to crumble, but he was aware that he had many people who wanted to help him. He told himself to stay calm when they reached the station to avoid unnecessary trouble. He accepted his fate and acknowledged his mistakes. He hoped that if the case went to trial, he would face a light sentence.

His heart ached for Aunt Sue, who had shielded him all those years. He was afraid that she would be considered an accomplice to his crime. He would make sure to spare Aunt Sue from prison. He could still remember when Aunt Sue ordered her staff to dismantle the blue sedan and burn the pieces. She hid what she had done from her children; only her husband knew, though he didn't agree. When she decided to move up north, he stayed behind. Her boys came with her, and Tom started his new life.

Sue's husband didn't ask for a divorce because he loved her more than his own life. But he couldn't tolerate her selfishness. Still, he stayed faithful to her. He felt lucky when the boys returned to him after college to start their careers. He visited them while they were separated and celebrated all of their accomplishments.

Tom's heart started to feel anxious the moment the police car stopped in the parking lot of the police station. His heartbeat was so fast that it felt like his heart would pop out from his chest and run faster than a race car. He could hear sirens and whistles.

25

MAMA BELLE WAS STILL CRYING. Vins held her hands; he was starting to calm down. Ivy reached for his arm and caressed him; she could feel his muscles harden under her touch. Vins wanted her hands all over him, but he ignored the thought.

Ivy's parents, brother, and Billy and Sam were cleaning up the mess in the dining room. They were all shaken by the chaos. When they were done, Daddy Todd made tea and coffee. The lawyer had given him his business card before he left, telling Daddy Todd to call him if they needed anything.

"Mama Belle, we will get justice for Papa now that his killer had been apprehended," Vins said "This will give us closure, and we can move on from that horrible incident."

Vins was whispering. He didn't want the others to hear what he was saying. His rage had subsided, and he wanted to focus on his next move: Tom's trial. Vins told his mother that he had made the biggest mistake of his life when he accused Ethan of being his father's killer. People had suffered because of his negligence.

"I'm sorry for your loss, hun," Ivy said. "Don't worry too much, Papa will have justice. I will make sure that my family doesn't interfere with the process. Mama Belle, I don't know how to console you, but you know I love you like you're my own mother. Please, let me know if you need anything?" Ivy's voice was soft and soothing, and Vins and Mama Belle knew that she really cared for them.

Ivy couldn't comprehend how this had happened to them. She had to consider the child in her tummy. The baby was Vins's flesh and blood, along with hers. Tom must pay the price for his mistakes. Ivy slowly softened her heart once again towards her husband. She knew he had his reasons for doing what he did; her support was what he needed now. Ivy could no longer hide her longing for Vins, and she held his hand while he continued to tell his story.

Vins began his confession. Ethan and Tom looked so similar that when Vins saw Ethan on television for the first time, he thought that Ethan was the man who had killed his father. He planned his revenge against Ethan, swearing that he would pay for what he had done.

When he had the opportunity to meet Ethan during one of his competitions the following year, Vins made sure that they were introduced. Then, he saw Ivy in the stands, cheering for Ethan along with their parents. He planned to deliberately pursue her. When they started dating, Vins didn't imagine that she would fall in love with him so quickly. His plan had worked; they were married, and he decided that he would continue his revenge on Ethan through Ivy. He saw that she was confident and successful, and he wanted to destroy her. Filing for divorce would be his final blow; seeing her devastation would destroy their family.

"Why are you making up all these stories, Vins?" Mama Belle said "I don't believe you. Was Ivy just collateral damage to you? She doesn't deserve all of this. You can't make her pay for her brother's mistakes." She was shouting, and she went to Ivy and hugged her. She felt awful about what her son had done.

"I'm sorry that he hurt you for the wrong reasons, my poor child," she said. "Please, I'm begging you to forgive him, but I would understand if you can't." Mama Belle was scared and desperate. Ivy was in shock; she moved away from Vins. Her brain couldn't understand what she was hearing, and she wanted to disappear.

"I wanted to hurt you because I thought Ethan was guilty of killing my father," Vins confessed.

"Now I know that wasn't true. Let's forget everything and start over again. Can you do that, Ivy, my wife? Your cousin and I both made a mistake. We're the same!" Vins felt relieved and his smirk is all over his face.

"Are you crazy?" Ivy said. "You want us to be together, in spite of all the evil things you've done to me?" Then she told them to leave and never come back into her life. Her whole body was shaking uncontrollably, and her tears keep falling. She held onto her belly; she wanted to run, but she couldn't move. Vins was surprised by her outburst. He wanted to touch her, but she told him to back off.

Her family heard Ivy yelling and barged into the living room. They saw her shaking and sobbing; her life had been crushed before their eyes, and her willpower was damaged beyond repair.

"You had no right to do that to me, Vins," she said. "My cousin killed your father in an accident, but you intentionally terminated our babies; that doesn't make you like Tom. He was young and had lost his parents when he accidentally committed that crime, but you intentionally destroyed my life and the lives of my unborn children. I will never forgive you for what you've done to me. As if I would forget everything after you've told me the truth. You are a manipulative bastard!"

Ivy couldn't control herself and continued to curse at Vins; she ignored Mama Belle's pleas. Her devotion to her husband had vanished into the thin air.

She had made the right decision in hiding her pregnancy from Vins. Right at that moment, she severed her ties with the Reynolds family. She felt sick to her stomach every time she recalled how Vins had lured her into marrying him, even though he never loved her. She had had enough of him; loving herself and her unborn child was her top priority from now on.

Ethan was at Ivy's side; her safety was his priority. How could he leave tomorrow?

"Stay away for now," he said to Vins. "Ivy is exhausted, and you need to deal with Tom. You have your own problems to solve. Stay away from my family." He couldn't believe this was happening to his sister.

"Come on, let's go to the police station," Robby said to Vins and Mama Belle. "We need to stay focused on Tom." He glared at Sam. "You need to think about how you conceived Brianna," he said. "As far as I know, I can't have children." He glanced at Billy.

Sam ignored him, turning to Billy, and reaching for his hands. Billy held her; his heart was beating fast. He was confused about what was happening to their entangled lives.

Mommy Nas and Daddy Todd stood between the living and dining rooms, their faces worried and tired. They chose not to say anything to Vins and Mama Belle.

Vins didn't want to leave; all he wanted was to hold his wife. He thought that if he told her the truth, she would understand. He stepped towards her, but Ethan blocked his way. Vins's mind couldn't accept the fact that this may be the last time he would see his wife. He had started to fall in love with Ivy. Before leaving, he looked at Ivy again and said, "Please don't give up on me Ivy, I'm begging you."

When Vins left, Mommy Nas instructed Ethan to carry Ivy upstairs, but she declined, telling them that she was pregnant not paralyzed. Ivy needed to be strong for herself and her baby. Sam and Billy went with her upstairs, leaving her family downstairs. Billy prepared a hot bath for Ivy and Sam picked out her night dress. Ivy said nothing. She lied on her bed and stared up at the ceiling, feeling numb and lonely. She had no idea how she was going to face the coming days and months, alone with a baby to take care of.

Sam called the nanny and asked her to bring the children to Ivy's house. She helped Ivy into the bath while Billy went downstairs to wait for the kids. Everything was calm now, but Billy knew that it was the calm before the storm.

Ethan called Marlon and asked him to hire security for Ivy's house, and that it would need to be in place before he left for Malaysia the following day. He also asked Marlon to hire a live-in nurse for his sister. His parents had agreed that they would also stay with Ivy until she was strong enough to face her new reality.

They had decided to hire security in case Vins showed up and caused trouble again. His mental state was unstable and the consequences of what he might do to Ivy were severe. Six more months and they would have their little bundle of joy. Thinking about the baby made them happy and excited.

The doorbell rang and the kids ran inside. The atmosphere in the house was instantly livelier. The children giggled and chatted about their adventures.

Mommy Nas and Daddy Todd would make sure that their grandchild would want for nothing. Being a single parent wasn't easy; Ivy was lucky to have her family and her two best friends as a support system.

26

IVY SIGNED THE DIVORCE PAPERS the next morning in front of her family and her two best friends. Nobody said anything. Ivy had no doubt that signing the papers would free her from harm. Her safety would be her first priority. Getting a divorce was the hardest decision she had ever made, but the best reward for herself and her baby.

Two personal bodyguards had arrived earlier along with the private nurse. Ethan made sure that he had provided Ivy with everything she needed to be safe at home before he left.

Paule arrived after Ethan had gone. Ivy had hired him to be her divorce lawyer. Then her parents left for the valley to prepare for their big move. They would return in three days' time.

Ivy asked Paule to join her in the study. He explained the procedures for filling for divorce. Ivy listened attentively. When they were done, Paule left to file the papers. Ivy felt relieved when she saw him leaving; there was no turning back. She had made the decision to give up on her marriage.

Ivy was not looking for love when she asked Paule to be her divorce lawyer. However, they started to spend a lot of time together because of the divorce, and she felt a connection to him. She sensed that he had strong feelings for her, and she couldn't deny that they had chemistry.

Paule had a charming way about him. She found him cute and alluring, and often caught him sneaking glances at her, which made her heart flutter. Still, she knew she had to avoid any relationship drama before her divorce from Vins was final. She had loved Vins so much, and she was carrying his baby.

During the divorce deliberations, Ivy did not ask for anything from Vins, but he learned about her pregnancy and wanted to give half of his assets to their child. He felt remorseful and wanted to make things right. Ivy had not once mentioned to him that her pregnancy was high-risk, and that she had no idea what was going to happen in the next six months. The judge considered the distribution of Vins's assets, and Ivy accepted the results. She was grateful to have Paule by her side during the proceedings.

Vins displayed an Oedipus complex; he had wanted to replace his father after he died. This made Ivy feel sick to her stomach.

Time passed, and Ivy's condition became stable. Mommy Nas stayed with her throughout her pregnancy. The nurse was great and made her life easier. The mother and daughter bonded well, and Ivy realized that her mom was getting ready to be a wonderful grandmother. She appreciated all the things that her mom did for her and her baby.

Ivy's parents came with her to her first ultrasound. When they reached the clinic, Daddy Todd felt sick and wanted to back out, but Mommy Nas told him he would regret it later. Finally, Daddy Todd came to his senses and went into the ultrasound room.

Mommy Nas sat beside Ivy and held her hand. Daddy Todd stood behind his wife with his hand on her shoulder. He patted Ivy's head and whispered in her ear, "I have no doubt that you will be the best mother to this baby."

When they heard the baby's heartbeat, Daddy Todd was the first to cry. Ivy looked at her Daddy and smiled at him. Mommy Nas didn't say a word; she squeezed her daughter's hand. Ivy instructed her doctor not to tell her the gender; she wanted to be surprised.

Ivy felt depressed many times throughout her pregnancy. She wanted to call Vins; she was yearning for his affection. Sometimes, she didn't think that she could raise a baby by herself. She felt scared and lonely, and just wanted to stay in bed. Mommy Nas was worried;

the nurse suggested they get Ivy out of the house for a walk, to distract her and raise her spirits.

Eventually, Ivy was able to go out and visit her friends and co-workers at the office. She was delighted; Sam made sure that Hannah hid how busy they were so that Ivy wouldn't be stressed.

The visit helped get Ivy back to her old self. Her dad left to take care of things at home; he visited weekly, then just once a month once things had settled down. Aunt Sue and Paule visited every time Sue was in town. She brought lots of gifts for Ivy's baby; Ivy accepted them but didn't want to offer Sue false hope that she and Paule would be together. She still felt that her love for Vins could never be replicated.

Tom went to trial and was convicted. He was tried as a minor; he was seventeen at the time of the accident. He was sentenced to two years in a minimum-security prison.

Tom made the best of his time in prison. He started a project called "Inmate Shirts for Change," where he used his skills and knowledge of the fashion industry to help his fellow inmates to design shirts that they could sell to support their transition out of prison. Ivy and Paule both helped him, and within three months they had sold nearly a thousand t-shirts.

Tom's time in prison made him a better person. He was calmer and less impulsive, with a greater appreciation for life. Ivy was glad that her cousin was changing for the better.

"My water broke!" Ivy said softly while holding her belly. Everyone hustle after hearing what Ivy said.

While at the hospital Ivy was immediately wheeled to the birthing room. Mommy Nas joined Ivy the entire duration of her delivery. Both Ivy and her mom were calm awaiting the birth of the baby.

The atmosphere outside the birthing room was stressful. Daddy Todd and Ethan were worried sick that something might happen to Ivy and her baby. Ivy's dad was so paranoid and couldn't stay still. Ethan was so nervous and anxious. Sam and Billy were concerned but hide their emotions from Daddy Todd and Ethan.

After ten hours of gruelling labour, the door of the birthing room opens, and Ivy's obstetrician came out and search for Ivy's family. Ethan and Daddy Todd approached her.

"Mr. Dacker, you need to light a cigar. You have a healthy and beautiful grandson!" The doctor said and patted Ethan's shoulder and congratulated them both, then left.

EPILOGUE

"HOW DO YOU WANT ME to deal with the funds that you got from your divorce, love?" Paule asked his fiancée. He had just gotten off the phone with his assistant, who had informed him of the results of the divorce proceedings.

Ivy looked at Paule lovingly; her eyes glowed every time she looked at him. He had become her rock and confidante since she signed her divorce papers two years ago.

She was breastfeeding Alfonso, who was eighteen months old. He got his father's lips, but other than that he was definitely Ivy's mini-me. Her pregnancy was difficult but made easier with the help of her support system. Paule had asked her to marry him two months after her divorce was final.

He had proposed the previous July during their annual summer get together at Pearwood Lane. Vins gave the house to Ivy for his son, and Ivy accepted it freely because she loved the house, even if it came with heartache and bad memories. She could imagine how Alfonso would enjoy this place along with Billy and Sam's children as they grew.

Ivy had no idea that Paule was planning to propose; they hadn't even dated or had a romantic relationship. But she was willing to open up her heart again and believe that her life would be different. Ivy said yes.

A week after the proposal, Ivy and Alfonso moved in with Paule. Before that, Ivy and her son had been staying at the lake house with a nanny and a driver/bodyguard. Ivy felt blessed that God had given her another chance at love, and a loving person to care for her son. Paule had gotten permission from her family and friends before he proposed.

Ethan told Paule to protect Ivy with his life and welcomed him to the family but warned him that Ivy had still been in love with Vins when Alfonso was born. Billy had given his blessing freely, but Sam had struggled. She couldn't stand to see her best friend go through so much pain again. But in the end, she also consented, telling Paule to love Ivy more than his own life.

Ivy was content and had a wonderful life with her son and Paule. She said yes to Paule because she saw how he treated Alfonso like his own. Accepting Alfonso as his own was the best gift Paule could give her.

Their winter wedding would be held at Tom's house on the North coast. Ivy and Paule had brought Alfonso to visit Tom when he was still in prison. He had fallen in love with the child and was glad that he would be free for the wedding. Paule told Ivy that Tom had included Alfonso in his will. However, when Tom offered Ivy a share in his company, Paule had declined. Ivy understood his decision and knew that he kept his jealousy at bay, which she found attractive.

Paule was soft-hearted towards his family, but he was one hell of a possessive man who didn't share what was his. He loved Tom as much as he loved Pierre, but Ivy was a different story. There would be no negotiation about her. Ivy couldn't stop smiling when she thought about it.

"Put the money from Vins in a trust fund for Alfonso," Ivy said. "He can access the money when he turns twenty-one. We must teach him to value money. His father may be difficult, but he worked hard for every penny he earned. Thank you for being with me through all this, Paule. You have made my life wonderful and I'm grateful that the universe surprised us and brought us together. I can't wait to marry you, love!"

Then they sealed it with a kiss.

DEDICATION

For my niece, Charlene Jaye, who encouraged me to
write this book by saying, "Why not?"

For my siblings, Donald, Joseph & Claire, Joanne,
and Leo John, for the unending support.

For Haydee and Natalie Christine, for being there for me.

For Nanay Beta, Mom, Dad, and Judy, your
spirit will always be with me.